"I will get you out of here, Gabriella. But I need to do my job, too."

Jaime leaned forward, his mouth so close Gabriella inhaled sharply, drowning a little in his dark eyes, wanting to get lost in the warm strength of his body.

He pulled his face away from hers, shaking his head. "I shouldn't—"

But Gabriella didn't want his "shouldn'ts" and she didn't want him to pull away, so she tugged Jaime closer and covered his mouth with hers.

Her tongue traced his mouth and she sighed against him. Melting, leaning. Crawling under all the defenses he wound around himself. False identities. Badges and pledges. Weapons and uniforms and lies. Even having dreamed of it, even in the midst of allowing it to happen in the here and now, Jaime knew it was wrong. Kissing Gabriella, drowning in it, was like taking advantage of her. It flew in the face of who he was as an FBI agent, as a law enforcement agent.

He should pull away. He should stop this madness. But he didn't stop. Couldn't. Because while it went against all those things he was, it didn't go against *who* he was. Deep down, this was what Jaime wanted…

Stone Cold Undercover Agent

NICOLE HELM

First Published in Great Britain 2013
By Mills & Boon, an imprint of HarperCollins*Publishers*
1 London Bridge Street, London SE1 9GF

Large Print edition 2017

© 2017 Nicole Helm

ISBN: 978-0-263-07240-2

Nicole Helm grew up with her nose in a book and the dream of one day becoming a writer. Luckily, after a few failed career choices, she gets to follow that dream—writing down-to-earth contemporary romance and romantic suspense. From farmers to cowboys, Midwest to *the* West, Nicole writes stories about people finding themselves and finding love in the process. She lives in Missouri with her husband and two sons and dreams of someday owning a barn.

The first romance novel I ever read
was a Romantic Suspense,
and I never thought I'd be able to
write one. Thank you, Helen and Denise,
for helping me prove past me wrong.

Chapter One

Gabby Torres had stopped counting the days of her captivity once it entered its sixth year. She didn't know why that was the year that did it. The first six had been painful and isolating and horrifying. She had lost everything. Her family. Her future. Her *freedom*.

The only thing she currently had was…life itself, which, in her case, wasn't much of a life when it came right down to it.

For the first four years of her abduction, she'd fought like a maniac. Anyone and anything that came near her—she'd attacked. Every time her captor got up close and told her some horrible thing, she'd fought in a way she had never known she could.

Maybe if the man hadn't so gleefully told her that her father was dead two years into her captivity, she might have eventually gotten tired of fighting. She might have accepted her fate as being some madman's kidnapping victim. But every time he appeared, she remembered how happily he had told her that her father had suffered a heart attack and died. It renewed her fight every single time.

But the oddest part of the eight years of captivity was that, though she'd been beaten on occasion in the midst of fighting back, mostly The Stallion and his men hadn't ever forced themselves on her or the other girls.

For years she'd wondered why and tried to figure out their reasoning…what their *point* was. Why she was there. Aside from the random jobs The Stallion forced her and the other girls to do, like sewing bags of drugs into car cushions or what have you.

But she was in year eight and tired of trying to figure out why she was there or what the point of it was. She was even tired of thinking about escape.

She'd been the first girl brought to the compound and, over the years, The Stallion had collected three more women. All currently existing in this boarded-up house in who knew where. Gabby had become something like the den mother as the new girls tried to figure out why they were there, or what they had done wrong, or what The Stallion wanted from them, but Gabby herself was done with wondering.

She had moved on. After she'd stopped counting every single day at year six, the past two years had been all about making this a reality. She kept track of Sundays for the girls and noted when a month or two had passed, but she had accepted this tiny, hidden-away compound as her life. The women were as much of a family as she was ever going to have, and the work The Stallion had them doing to hide drugs or falsify papers was her career.

Accepting at this point was all she could do. If sometimes her brain betrayed her as she tried to fall asleep, or one of the girls muttered something about escape, she pushed it down and out as far as it would go.

Hope was a cancer here. All she had was acceptance.

So when just another uncounted day rolled around and The Stallion, for the first time in all of those days, brought a man with him into her room, Gabby felt an icy pierce of dread hit her right in the chest.

Though she'd accepted her fate, she hadn't

accepted *him*. Perhaps because no matter how eight years had passed, or how he might disappear for months at a time, or the fact he never touched her, he seemed intent on making her *break*.

Quite honestly, some days that's what kept her going. Making sure he never knew he'd broken her of hope.

So, though she had accepted her lot—or so she told herself—she still dreamed of living longer than him and airing all his dirty laundry. Outliving him and making sure he knew he had never, *ever* broken her. She very nearly smiled at the thought of him dead and gone. "So, who are you?"

The man who stood next to The Stallion was tall, broad and covered in ominous black. Black hair—both shaggy on his head and bearded on his face—black sunglasses, black shirt and jeans. Even the weapons, mostly guns, he had strapped all over him were black. Only his skin tone wasn't black, though it was a dark olive hue.

"I told you she was a feisty one. Quite the fiery little spitball. She'll be perfect for you," The Stallion said, his smile wide and pleased with himself.

The icy-cold dread in Gabby's chest delved deeper, especially as this new man stared at her from somewhere behind his sunglasses. Why was he wearing sunglasses in this dark room? It wasn't like she had any outside light peering through the boarded window.

He murmured something in Spanish. But Gabby had never been fluent in her grandparents' native language and she could barely pick out any of the words since he'd spoken them so quickly and quietly.

The Stallion's cold grin widened even further. "Yes. Have lots of fun with her. She's all yours. Just remember the next time I ask you for a favor that I gave you exactly what you specified. Enjoy."

The Stallion slid out of the room, and the ominous click of the door's lock nearly made Gabby jump when no sounds and nothing in her life had made her jump for nearly two years.

While The Stallion's grin was very nearly... psychotic, as though he'd had some break with reality, the man still in her room was far scarier. He didn't smile in a way that made her think he was off in some other dimension. His smile was... Lethal. Ruthless. *Alive.*

It frightened her and she had given up fear a very long time ago.

"You don't speak Spanish?" he asked with what sounded almost like an exaggerated accent. It didn't sound like any of the elderly people in her family who'd grown up in Mexico, but then, maybe his background wasn't Mexican.

"No, not really. But apparently you speak English, so we don't have a problem."

"I guess that depends on your definition of problem," he said, his voice low and laced with threat.

What Gabby wanted to do was to scoot back on the bed as far into the corner as she possibly could, but she had learned not to show her initial reactions. She had watched The Stallion get far too much joy out of her flight responses in the beginning, and she'd learned to school them away. So even though she thought about it, even though she pictured it in her head complete with covering her face with her hands and cowering, she didn't do it. She stayed exactly where she was and stared the man down.

He perused the bedroom that had been her life for so long. Oh, she could go anywhere in the small, boarded-up house, but she'd learned to appreciate her solitude even in captivity.

The man opened the dresser drawers and pawed through them. He inspected the baseboards and slid his large, scarred hands up and down the walls. He even pulled at the boards over the windows.

"Measuring for drapes?" she asked as sarcastically as she could manage.

The man looked at her, still wearing his sunglasses, which she didn't understand at all. His lips curved into an amused smile. It made Gabby even more jumpy because, usually, the guards The Stallion had watching them weren't the brightest. Or maybe they'd had such rough lives they didn't care for humor of any kind. Either way, very few people, including the women she lived with, found her humor funny.

He was back to his perusal and there was

a confident grace about him that made no sense to her. He wasn't like any of the other men she'd come into contact with during her captivity. He was handsome, for starters. She couldn't think of one guard who could probably transfer from a life of crime into a life of being a model, but this man definitely could.

It made all of her nerves hum. It gave her that little tingle that mysteries always did—the idea that if she paid enough attention, filed enough details away, she could solve it. Figure out why he was different before he did her any harm.

She'd begun to wonder if she hadn't gone a little crazy when she noticed these things no one else seemed to. She was pretty sure Tabitha thought she was out of her mind for having theories about The Stallion's drug and human trafficking operations. For coming up with a theory that he spent three months there and split the other seasons at three other houses that would ostensibly be just like this one.

She'd been here for eight years and she knew his patterns. She was sure of it. Things puzzled together in her head until it all made sense. But the girls all looked at her like she was crazy for coming up with such ideas, so she'd started keeping them to herself. She'd started trying to stop her brain from acting.

But it always did and maybe she had gone completely and utterly insane. Eight years ago her life had been ripped away from her, but she didn't even get to be dead. She had to be here living in this weird purgatory.

Wouldn't that drive anyone to the brink of insanity? Maybe her patterns and theories were gibberish.

Finally the man had looked through everything in the room except her bed where she was currently sitting. He advanced on her with easy, relaxed strides that did nothing to calm the tenseness in her muscles or the heavy beating of her heart. She couldn't remember the last time in her captivity she'd felt so afraid.

He didn't say anything and she couldn't see his eyes underneath the sunglasses, so whatever he was thinking or feeling was a blank-expressioned mystery.

Finally, after a few humming seconds, he lifted a long finger up to the ceiling. She frowned at him and he made the gesture again until she realized he wanted her to get off the bed.

Since most of the guards' preferred way of getting her to do something was to grab her and throw her around, she supposed she should feel more calm with this man who hadn't yet touched her.

But she wasn't calm. She didn't trust him at all.

She did get up off the bed and, instead of scurrying away, tried to measure her steps and very carefully move to the farthest corner from him.

The man lifted every single blanket on her bed and then, in an easy display of muscles, the heavy mattress and box spring, as well. He got down on all fours and looked under the bed and, finally, she realized he was searching for something in particular.

She just had no idea what on earth he could be looking for.

"No bugs?"

She stared at him. What, did he have some weird fear of ladybugs or ants or something? Then she realized the intensity with which he was staring at her and recalled how carefully he had looked through every inch of this little room. Yeah, he wasn't looking for insects.

"I've been here for eight years. As far as I

know, he's never bugged or videotaped individual rooms."

The man raised his eyebrows. "But he films other rooms?"

Gabby trusted this man almost less than she trusted The Stallion, which was not at all. She offered a careless shrug. The last thing she was going to do was to share all of her ideas and information with this stranger.

"Tell me about your time here."

There was a gentleness to his tone that didn't fool her at all. "Tell me who you are."

He smiled again, an oddly attractive smile that was so out of place in this dire situation. "The Stallion told me you'd be exactly what I was looking for. I don't think he knew just how perfect you'd be."

"Perfect for what?" she demanded, trying to keep the high-pitched fear out of her voice.

"Well, he thinks you'd be the perfect payment. A high-spirited fighter—the kind of woman who would appeal to my baser instincts."

This time Gabby couldn't stop herself from pushing back into the corner or cowering. For the first year she'd been held captive, she'd been sure she'd be sexually assaulted. She'd never heard about an abduction that hadn't included that, not that she'd had any deep knowledge of abductions before.

But no one had ever touched her that way and she'd finally gotten to a point where she didn't think it would happen. That was her own stupid fault for thinking this could be her normal.

The man finally took off his sunglasses. His eyes were almost as dark as his hair, a brown that was very nearly black. Everything about his demeanor changed; the swagger, the suave charm, gone.

"I'm not going to hurt you," he said in a low voice.

Maybe if she hadn't been a captive for eight years, she might have believed him. But she didn't, not for a second.

"You're just going to need to play along," he continued in that maddeningly gentle voice.

"Play along with what?" she asked, pushing as far into the corner as she could.

"You'll see."

Gabby wanted to cry, which had been an impulse she'd beaten out of herself years ago, but it was bubbling up inside her along with the new fear. It wasn't fair. She was so tired of her life not being fair.

When the man reached out for her, she went with those instincts from the very first time she'd been brought there.

She fought him with everything she had.

JAIME ALESSANDRO HADN'T worked his way up "The Stallion's" operation by being a particularly *nice* guy. Undercover work, especially this long and this deep, had required him to bend a lot of the moral codes he'd started police work with.

But thus far, he'd never had to beat up or restrain a woman. This woman was surprisingly agile and strong, and she was coming at him with everything she had.

He was very concerned he was going to have to hurt her just to get her to stop. He could stand a few scratches, but he doubted The Stallion was going to trust him with the next big job if he let this woman give him a black eye— no matter how strong and "feisty" she was.

God, how he hated that word.

"Ma'am." He tried for his forceful FBI agent voice as he managed to hold one of her arms still. He didn't want to hurt the poor woman who'd been here eight years—a fact he only knew because she'd just told him.

He shouldn't have been surprised at this point. He'd learned very quickly in his undercover work that what the FBI had on Victor Callihan, a.k.a. The Stallion, was only the tip of the iceberg.

If he thought about it too much, the things The Stallion had done, the things Jaime had done to get here... Well, he didn't, because he'd had to learn how to turn that voice of right and wrong off and focus only on the task at hand.

Bringing down The Stallion.

That meant if she didn't stop flailing at him and landing some decent blows, he was going to have to restrain her any way he could, even if it caused her some pain.

Though he had her arm clamped in a tight grip, she still thrashed and kicked at him, very nearly landing a blow that would have brought him to his knees. He swore and, though he very much didn't want to, gave her a little jerk that gave him the leverage he needed to grab her from behind with both arms.

She still bucked and kicked, but with his height advantage and a full grip on her upper body, he could maneuver her this way and that to keep her from landing any nasty hits.

"I'm not going to hurt you. I'm going to help you, I promise."

She spat, probably aiming for him but missing completely since he had her from behind. It was only then he realized he'd spoken in Spanish instead of English.

He'd grown up speaking both, but his work for The Stallion and the identity he'd assumed required mostly speaking Spanish and pretending he struggled with English.

It was slipups like that—not realizing what

language he was speaking, not quite remembering who he was—that always sent a cold bolt of fear through him.

He needed this to be over. He needed to get out. Before he lost himself completely. He could only hope that Gabriella Torres would be the last piece of the puzzle in getting to the heart of The Stallion's operation.

"I'm not going to hurt you," Jaime said in a low, authoritative tone. Certain, self-assured, even though he didn't feel much of either at this particular moment.

"Then let go of me," she returned, still bucking, throwing her head back and narrowly missing head-butting him pretty effectively.

He tried not to think about what might have happened to her in the course of being hidden way too long from the world. It was a constant fight between the human side of him and the role he had to play. He wouldn't lose his humanity, though. He refused. He might have to bend his moral code from time to time, but he wouldn't lose the part of him that would feel sympathy. If he lost that, he'd never be able to go back.

Jaime noted that though Gabriella still fought his tight hold, she was tiring.

"Be still and I'll let you go," he said quietly, hoping that maybe his outer calm would rub off on her.

She tried to land a heel to his shin but when that failed she slumped in his arms. "Fine."

Carefully and slowly, paying attention to the way she held herself and the pliancy of her body, Jaime released her from his grip. Since she didn't renew her fight, he took a few steps away so she could see he had no intention of hurting her.

When she turned and looked at him warily, he held his hands up. Her breathing was labored and there were droplets of sweat gathered at her temples. She had a pretty face despite the pallor beneath her tan complexion. She had a mass of dark curls pulled back and away from her face, and he had to wonder how old she was.

She looked both too young and too worldweary all at the same time, but he couldn't let that twist his insides. He'd seen way worse at this point, hadn't he? "I'm not going to harm you, Gabriella. In fact, I want to help you."

She laughed, something bitter and scathing that scraped against what little conscience he had left.

"Sure you do, buddy. And this is the Taj Mahal."

Yeah, she'd be perfect for what he needed. Now he just had to figure out how to use her without blowing everything he'd worked for.

Chapter Two

Gabby was wrung out. Physically. Emotionally. It had been a long time since she'd had something to react so violently against. Her breathing was uneven and her insides felt scraped raw.

She wanted to cry and it had been so long since she'd allowed herself that emotional release.

She couldn't allow it now. Not with the way this man studied her, intently and far too interested. She had become certain of her power in this odd world she'd been thrust into against her will, but she didn't believe in that power in the face of this man.

She closed her eyes against the wave of despair and the *need* to give up on this whole *surviving* thing.

"Gabriella. I know you have no reason to trust me, but I'm going to say it even if you don't believe it. I will not hurt you."

The worst part was that she was so exhausted she *wanted* to believe him. No one had promised her safety in the past eight years, but just because no one had didn't mean she could believe this one.

"I guess it's my lucky day," she returned, trying to roll her eyes but exhaustion limited the movement.

"I know. I know. I do. Don't trust me. Don't believe. I just need you to go along with some things."

"What kind of things? And, more important,

why?" She shook her head. Questions were pointless. The man was going to lie to her anyway. "Never mind. It doesn't matter. Do whatever you're going to do."

"You fought me."

"So?"

He stepped forward and she stumbled away. He shook his head, holding his hands up again, as if surrendering. "I'm sorry. I won't. I'm not going to touch you." He kept his hands raised as he spoke. Low, with a note to his voice she couldn't recognize.

Panic? No, he wasn't panicked in the least. But there was something in that tone that made her feel like time was running out. For what, she had no idea. But there was a *drive* to this man, a determination.

He had a goal of some kind and it wasn't like The Stallion's goals. The Stallion had a kind of meticulous nature, and he never seemed rushed or driven. Just a cold, careful, step-by-step map in his head to whatever endgame he had. Or maybe no endgame at all. Just… living his weird life.

But *this* man in her room had a vitality to him, an energy. He was trying to *do* something and Gabby hated the way she responded to that. Oh, she missed having a goal, having some *fight* in her. The weary acceptance of the past two years had given her less and less to live for. Helping the other girls was the only thing that kept her getting up every morning.

"What do you want from me?"

"Just some cooperation. Some information. To go along with whatever I say, especially if The Stallion is around."

"Are you trying to usurp him or something?"

He released a breath that was almost a laugh. "N—" He seemed to think better of saying no. "Who knows? Right now, I need information."

"Why should I give you anything?"

He seemed to think about the question but in the end ignored it and asked one of his own. "Is it true…?" He trailed off, giving her a brief once-over. "They haven't touched you while you've been here?"

She stared hard at the man. "One time a guard tried to touch my chest and I knocked his tooth out."

The man's full mouth curved a little at that, something so close to humor in his expression it hurt. Humor. She missed…laughing. For no reason. Smiling, just because it was a nice day with a blue sky.

But she couldn't think about all the things she missed or her heart would stop beating.

"What happened to the guard?"

Gabby shrugged, hugging herself against all this *feeling*. Thoughts about laughter, about the sky, about using her mind to put the pieces of the puzzle together again.

You gave that up. You've accepted your fate.

But had she, really, when the fight came so easily and quickly?

"I don't know. I never saw him again."

"Was it only the one time?"

Gabby considered how much information she wanted to give a stranger who might be just as evil as the man who held her captive. She could help him boot The Stallion out…and then get nothing for her trouble. She wasn't sure if she preferred to take the risk. The devil you knew and all that.

But there was something about this man… He didn't fit. Nothing about his demeanor or mannerisms or his questions fit the past eight years of her experience. What exactly would be the harm in telling him what she knew?

What would The Stallion do? He'd been the one to leave her with this man.

"As far as I know, they can knock us around as long as they don't break anything or touch our faces. If they go overboard, or get sexual, they disappear."

The man raised an eyebrow. "How many have disappeared?"

Gabby shrugged, still holding herself. "It was more in the beginning. Five the first year. Three the second. Only one in the third. Then five again the fourth. Two the fifth, then none since."

Both his eyebrows raised at this point, his eyes widening in surprise. "You remember it that specifically?"

Part of her wanted to brag about all the things she remembered. All the specifics she had locked away in her brain. All the patterns she'd put together. None of the girls had ever appreciated them. She had a feeling this man would.

But it would be showing her hand a little too easily for comfort. "Not a lot to think about in this place. I remember some things."

"Tell me," he said, taking another one of those steps toward her that made her want to cower or run away to whatever corner she could find. But she stood her ground and she shook her head.

If she told him, it would be in her own time, when she thought telling might work in her favor in some way.

He stood there, opposite her, studying her face as though he could figure out how to get her to talk if he simply looked hard enough.

So she looked right back, trying to determine something about *him*.

He had a sharp nose and angular cheekbones, a strong jaw covered liberally with short, black whiskers. His eyes looked much less black close up, a variety of browns melding to the black pupil at the center.

He had broad shoulders and narrow hips and even the array of weapons strapped to him didn't detract from the sexy way he was built. Sexy. Such an odd thing. She hadn't thought about sex or attractiveness or much of anything in that vein for eight long years.

She didn't know if she was glad she could still see it and recognize it or if it just made everything more complicated. Far more lonely.

The eerie click of a lock interrupted the moment and he looked back at the door, then at her. His expression was grave.

"I'm not going to hurt you," he whispered. "But this may scare you a little bit. That's okay. Fight back."

"Fight ba—"

He reached out and grabbed her by the shirt

with both large hands. She screeched, but he had her shirt ripped in two before she landed the first punch.

JAIME PRETENDED TO laugh as Gabby pounded at him. He glanced at The Stallion, doing his best to stand between the man and his view of Gabby. He'd tried not to look himself, but he needed the illusion of a fight. A sexual one.

He couldn't let his disgust at that show. *"Senor?"* The Stallion always got some bizarre thrill when Jaime called him that, so he'd done it with increasing regularity. Being the egomaniac that he was, The Stallion never got tired of it. "An hour, no?"

"I'm sorry to interrupt, but I need you immediately. Your hour will have to wait."

Jaime scowled. He didn't have to fake it, either. He wanted more information from Gabriella. If the woman had remembered how many guards were dismissed every year...who knew what other kind of information she might have.

Jaime inclined his head as if he agreed, though he didn't at all. He wanted to get information out of Gabriella as soon as possible. The more he got and the sooner he got it, the less he'd have to do for The Stallion.

He gave her a fleeting glance. Those big, dark eyes were edged with fury, and she crossed her arms over her chest. The bra she wore was ill-fitting and he couldn't help but notice the way her breasts spilled over the fabric even under her crossed arms.

He quickly looked back at The Stallion. He handed Gabriella the remains of her shirt. *"Perdón,"* he offered, making sure he didn't sound sorry in the least.

The Stallion chuckled as Jaime walked to meet him at the door. "You could be so much better at your job if you weren't so easily distracted," the man said, clapping him on the shoulder in an almost fatherly manner as he pulled the door closed, leaving Gabby alone in the room.

He didn't lock the door this time and Jaime was surprised at how much freedom he allowed the women he kept there. Of course, the front and back doors were chained and locked even when The Stallion was inside, and all the windows were boarded up in a permanent, meticulous manner.

There were no phones in the house, no computers. Absolutely no technology of any kind aside from kitchen appliances. But even that was relegated to a microwave and a refrigerator. No stove and no knives beyond dull butter ones.

He wondered if the women inside knew that only a couple of yards away, in a decent-size shed, The Stallion kept all the things he denied the women. Computers and phones and an array of weapons, which was where The Stallion was leading Jaime now.

"We have a situation I want you briefed on. Then you may go back to our Gabriella and finish your…" He trailed off and shook his head as he locked and chained the back door they'd exited into an overgrown backyard. "Sex is such a *base* instinct, Rodriguez. Women are a worthless expense of energy. I'm fifty-three, for over half my life I have searched for the perfect woman and failed time and time again. Though, I will admit the women I've kept are of exceptional quality. Just not quite there…"

The man got a far-off look on his face as they walked through the long grass toward his shed. It was the kind of far-off look that kept Jaime up at night. Void of reason or sense, completely and utterly…incomprehensible.

The Stallion patted his shoulder again, tsking. "I know this is all going over your head. You really ought to work on your English."

Jaime shrugged. It suited his purpose to be seen as not understanding everything that went on because of a language barrier, and at times it had been hard to remember he was supposed to barely understand.

But when The Stallion started going on and on about women, Jaime never had any problems keeping his mouth shut and his expression confused. It was broken and warped and utter nonsense.

The Stallion unlocked the shed and stepped inside. Two men were sitting on chairs around The Stallion's desk, which was covered in notes and technology. The man strode right to it and sat on his little throne.

"Herman's gone missing," he said without preamble, mentioning The Stallion's most used runner in Austin. "He didn't deliver his message today, and so far no one has figured out where he disappeared to. Wallace, I'm giving you the rest of today to find him. He can't have gone too far."

The fair-haired man in the corner nodded soundlessly.

"If he *somehow* gives us the slip that long…" The Stallion continued. "Layne, you'll take him out."

Layne cracked his knuckles one by one, like he'd seen too many mobster movies. "Be my pleasure. What happens to him if Wallace finds him, though? I wouldn't mind getting some information out of him."

The Stallion's mouth curved into a cold, menacing line that, even after two years, made Jaime's blood run cold. "Rodriguez will be in charge if we find him. I'd like to see what he can do with a…shall we say, recalcitrant employee. *¿Comprende?*"

"Sí, senor."

"Wallace, you're dismissed. Report every hour," The Stallion said with the flick of his wrist. "Layne, have the interrogation room readied for us, please."

Both men agreed and left the shed. Jaime stood as far from The Stallion as he could without drawing attention to the purposeful space between them. The man steepled his hands together, looking off at some unknown entity Jaime was pretty sure only he could see.

Jaime stood perfectly still, trying to appear detached and uninterested. "Did you need me, *senor*?"

The Stallion stroked his forehead with the back of his thumb, still looking somewhere else. "Once we figure out what's going on with Herman, I'll be moving on to a different location." His cold, blue gaze finally settled on Jaime. "You'll stay here and hold down the fort, and Ms. Gabriella will be yours to do whatever you please with her."

Jaime smiled. "Excellent." He didn't have to fake his excitement about that, because Jaime was almost certain Gabriella had exactly the information he'd need to pull the sting to end this whole nightmare of a job.

And then Jaime could go back to being himself and figuring out…who that was again.

Chapter Three

Gabby considered taking a nap in lieu of lunch. Her little *visit*, which she couldn't begin to understand, however, had eradicated any appetite she'd had.

That man had acted like two different people. Even the way he talked when The Stallion was present and when he wasn't was different. His voice, when he'd spoken with her, had only the faintest touches of Mexico, reminding her of her parents' accents—a sharp, hard pang of memory.

But when he spoke to The Stallion, it was all

rolled R's and melodic vowels. Even his demeanor had changed. That goal or determination or whatever she thought she'd seen in him just…disappeared in the shadow of The Stallion. He was someone else. Something more feral and menacing.

But, despite the very disconcerting shirt-ripping, and the way his gaze had most definitely lingered on her chest, he had been honest with her thus far.

He hadn't hurt her, but he'd let her hurt him. Blow after blow. Considering she'd gotten into the habit of exercising to keep her overactive mind from driving her crazy, she wasn't weak. She had punched him with everything she had, and though he hadn't made too much of an outward reaction, it had to have hurt.

She shook away the thoughts, already tired of the merry-go-round in her head. If she couldn't nap or eat, she'd do the next best thing. Exercise until she was too exhausted to think or to move or to do anything but sleep.

She rolled to the ground, then pushed up, holding the plank position as she counted slowly. It had become a game, to see how long she could hold herself up like this. The counting kept her brain from circling and the physical exertion helped her sleep better.

A knock sounded at the door, which was odd. No one here knocked. Except the girls, but that was rare and only in case of emergency.

Before she could stand or say anything, the door squeaked open and in stepped the man from earlier.

She scowled at him. "I only have so many clothes, so if you're going to keep ripping them, at least get me some duct tape or something."

He pulled the door closed as he stepped inside. "I won't rip your clothes again...unless I have to." He studied her arms, eyebrows pulling together. "You're awfully strong."

"Remember that."

"It could definitely work in our favor," he muttered. "Now, where were we?"

She pushed into a standing position. "You don't want to go back to where we were. I'll hit you where it *really* hurts this time." Why he smiled at that was completely beyond her.

"You might literally be perfect."

"And you might literally be as whacked as Mr. Stallion out there."

He shook his head in some kind of odd rebuttal. "Now—"

"You act like two very different people."

He froze, every part of his body tensing as his eyes widened. "What?"

"You act like two completely different people. In here alone. With him. Two separate identities."

He was so still she wasn't even sure he breathed.

"Two separate identities, huh?"

"Your accent is different when he's not here. The way you hold yourself? It's more…relaxed when he's with you. Rigid with me. No…almost…" She cocked her head, trying to place it. "Military."

She knew she was getting somewhere at the way he still didn't move, though he'd carefully changed his wide-eyed gaze into something blank.

Yeah, she was right. "You were military."

"No."

"Police then?"

"You're an odd woman, Gabriella." He said her name with the exaggerated accent, and it reminded her of her long-dead grandfather. He hadn't been a particularly nice man or a particularly mean man. He'd been hard. Very formal. And while everyone else in her family had called her Gabby, he'd been the lone holdout.

He'd never appreciated the "Americanization" of his family, even though he'd immigrated as a young man.

"I'm right. You're…" Her eyes widened as she put it all together. Him not hurting her. Him gathering information. Being someone else with The Stallion.

He gave a sharp head shake so she didn't say anything, but she did step closer. "But you are, aren't you?"

"No," he returned easily, nodding his head as he said it.

Her heart raced, her breathing came too shallow. He was an undercover police officer. She had to blink back tears. "Tell me what it means, that you're here. Please."

He let out a long breath and stepped toward

her. This time she didn't scurry away. She needed to know more than she was afraid of him. He'd checked the room for bugs before, and she knew they were safe to talk in there, but she also understood how a man like him would have to be inordinately careful. *Undercover.* What did it mean? For her? For the girls?

He inclined his mouth toward her ear, so close she could feel his breath against her neck. "I can't promise you anything. I can only tell you that I am trying to end this, so whatever information you can give me, whatever you can tell me, it'll bring me closer to finishing out my job here."

He pulled back, looking at her, his gaze serious and that determination back in his dark eyes.

She tried to repeat those first five words. *I can't promise you anything.* It was important to remember, to not get her hopes up. Just be-

cause he was an undercover police officer…
just because he wanted to take The Stallion
down…it didn't mean he *would*. Or that he'd
get her out in the process.

"How did you put it all together?" he asked.
"I'm not…"

"You're very good. Very convincing. I'm
probably the only person you let your guard
down for, right?"

He nodded, still clearly perplexed and downright worried she'd figured it out.

"I don't know, ever since I got here…I remember things, and I can see…patterns that
no one else seems to see. I thought I was going
crazy. But…I don't know. I was always good
at that. Observing, remembering, figuring
out puzzles and mysteries. It just works in my
head."

"Clearly," he muttered. "Hopefully you're

the only one around here with that particular talent or I'm screwed."

"How long?" she asked. Was he just starting out? He was so close to The Stallion, surely...

"Two years."

She let out a breath. "That's a long time."

"Yes," he said, a bleak note in his voice that softened her another degree toward him. He'd voluntarily held his own identity hostage, separated himself from his life. He'd probably had no idea the things he'd end up missing or wanting.

God help her, she hadn't had a clue in that first day, week, month, even year. She'd had no idea the things that would grow to hurt her.

She felt a wave of sympathy for the man and, even if it was stupid or ill-advised, she had to follow it. She had to follow this first possibility in *ages* that there might be an end to this. "How can I help?"

"So, you trust me?"

"I don't trust anyone anymore," she returned, feeling a little bleak herself. "But I'll try to help you. Because I believe you are what I think you are."

"That'll work. That'll work. But there's something you have to understand. Being a different person means being a *different* person. The ripping-your-shirt thing…"

"It was for him to think that you were…having your way with me." She shuddered a little at the thought, at how close they might have to come to…proving that.

"Yes. There may be times I have to push that a little bit. Because he is…" He cleared his throat. "What do you understand about your position here? Is there a reason you were kidnapped? Is there a reason he's kept you girls… untouched?"

"I'm not really sure. I have no idea why I was

taken. I was waiting at my dad's work for him to get off his shift and all of a sudden there were all these people and men talking and I was grabbed and thrown into a van with some other people. They took us somewhere that I don't know anything about. It was all dark and sometimes we were blindfolded or there were hoods put on our heads."

Gabby felt ill. She didn't relive the kidnapping anymore. She'd mostly gotten beyond *that* horror and lived in the horror of her continual imprisonment. Going back and thinking about coming here brought up all sorts of horrible memories.

How awful she'd been to her mother that night when she'd had to cancel her date to pick up Dad. All that fear she hadn't known what to do with or how to survive with when she'd been taken, moved, inspected. But she had.

She had survived and lived, and she needed to remind herself of that.

"Eventually, after I don't know how long… Actually that's not true." She didn't have to lie to this man about her memory or pretend she didn't know exactly what she knew like she did with so many people. "It was two days. It was two days from the time they took me and put me in the van to the time they took me to this other place, kind of like a warehouse. They took me—and all the people from that first moment—there and then we were sorted. Men and women went to different areas. And then The Stallion came."

"Keep going," he urged, and it was only then she realized she'd stopped because she could see it. Relive every terrifying detail of not knowing what would happen to her, or why.

"I didn't know that's who he was at the time, but he walked through and he asked everyone if we knew who he was. One woman in my group said yes and she was immediately taken away."

"Did he say his name or offer any hints about who he was beyond The Stallion?"

"No. I've gone over it a million times in my head. He must've…he must be someone, you know? He had to be someone with some kind of profile?"

"Yes, he is."

"He is?" She stepped toward the man who could mean freedom, a scary thought in and of itself. "Who? What's his name? Why is he doing this?" she demanded, losing her cool and her calm in an instant.

"I can't answer those questions."

She grabbed his shirtfront, desperate for an answer, a reason, desperate for those things she'd finally given up on ever getting. "Tell me right this second, you miserable—"

"I'm sorry," he said so gently, so *emotionally*, she could only swallow a sob.

"He kidnapped me. He brought me here. He separated me from my family for eight years, and you can't tell me who he is?" she demanded, her voice low and scratchy but measured. She was keeping it together. She would keep it together.

"Not now. There are a lot of things I can't tell you, because everything you know jeopardizes what I'm doing here. You deserve the answers, you do, but I can't give you what you deserve right now. But if you help me, you'll have the answers, and you'll have your *life* back."

Odd *that* prompted a cold shudder to go through her body. "You can't promise me that."

"No, I can't, but I promise to put my life on the line to make it so."

She didn't know what to do with that or him,

or any of this, so she turned away from him, hugging herself, trying to calm her breathing.

There were no promises. There were no guarantees. But she had a *chance*. She had to believe in it. She had to *fight* for it. With everything she had. If not for herself, for the three girls she shared this hell with. For their family's, and hers, even if they probably thought she was dead.

She owed it to a lot of people to do what this man said he would do: put her life on the line to make it so.

GABRIELLA WAS CLEARLY BRILLIANT. The way she described remembering things and figuring out patterns no one else did, to the point she thought she was crazy… It sounded like a lot of the analysts he knew. Because when you saw things no one else saw, it was very easy to convince yourself you were wrong.

But she wasn't wrong, and she had *so* much information in that pretty head of hers… Jaime was nearly excited even though she now had the power to end his life completely.

He didn't care because he was so close now. So damn close to the end of this.

She might be brilliant, but he was a trained FBI agent, after all. He wasn't going to let her figuring him out be the end. No way in hell.

"Tell me about what happened after the woman who knew who he was disappeared."

Gabriella nodded. "She was taken away from the room. She had no chance to say anything at all. After that, the rest of us women were separated into groups, and I tried to find a rhyme or reason for these groups, but I really couldn't. Except that all of the women in my group were young and reasonably fit. Dark hair, though none of the same shade—it ranged from black to light brown."

Jaime thought back to The Stallion's odd statement about searching half his life for the perfect woman. He couldn't make sense of it, but that had to be connected to this.

"At that point, it was just six of us. The Stallion lined us up and, one by one, he inspected us."

"Inspected you how?"

Gabriella visibly shuddered, and Jaime hated that she had to relive this, but she did. If they were going to put The Stallion away, she'd probably have to relive it quite frequently.

"He touched our hair and…smelled it." She audibly swallowed, hugging herself so tightly he wished he could offer some comfort, some support.

But he was nothing to her.

"He had one of his cronies measure us."

"Measure you?"

"You know, like if you've ever been measured for clothes?" She turned to face him again, though her dark eyes were averted. But she gestured to her body as she spoke. "Shoulders, arms, chest, hips, legs, inseam, and the guy yelled out each number and The Stallion wrote it all down on this little notepad."

She was quiet for a few seconds and instead of pushing this time, he let her gain her composure, let her take the time she needed.

Time wasn't on his side, but he couldn't… lose the humanity. That was his talisman. *Don't lose your humanity.*

"He dismissed everyone except me."

Jaime didn't know how to absorb that. He could picture it too easily after everything he'd done with and for The Stallion. The fear she must have felt having been taken for no reason, having been chosen for no reason that she understood.

It was dangerous to fill her in on the things he knew. But he had already entered dangerous territory when he had allowed himself to behave differently enough with her for her to figure out who he was. *What* he was.

"He's a sick man," Jaime offered.

"A sick man who is very, very smart or very, very lucky since he hasn't gotten caught in eight years. Probably more than that."

"Yes. Listen, there are a lot of things The Stallion does. But this thing you're involved in… He told me something just now about how he spent over half his life looking for the perfect woman. That women are basically stupid and you shouldn't dirty yourself with them unless you find this perfect specimen."

"Oh, how lovely. I'd love to show him how *stupid* I can be. With my fists."

He smiled at the irritation in her tone because it was *life*. A spark. It wasn't that shaky fear that had taken over as she had relived her kidnapping experience.

"Let him have his delusions. They might get

us out of this mess." He wanted to reach out and take her shoulders or…something. Something to cement this partnership, but he was still a strange man in her room who'd ripped her shirt. He had to be careful. Human. "Between what you said and he said, I think that's what he's been doing with this arm of things. Searching for the perfect woman."

"So that's what the measuring was, then. He has a perfect size, I just bet." Gabriella rolled her eyes. "Disgusting pig. And then when we got here he, like, tested me. He would ask these questions, and I never answered. I only fought. For weeks, every time he opened his mouth, I'd just attack. I thought maybe that's why…"

She took in a shaky breath, still hugging herself. Jaime hadn't been lying when he'd said she might be perfect. She was smart, she was strong—not just physically. Strong at her core.

"I thought for sure I would be raped, but I never have been, and I've never understood why."

"He thinks women are dirty. At least, in this context of looking for the perfect woman. I can't rationalize a madman, but the point is that you were brought here because he thought you *could* be the perfect woman. The fighting, I guess, proved to him that you weren't."

"I thought that for the longest time, but that isn't it. Jasmine—she was brought here my second year—she didn't fight him at all. She told him she'd do whatever he wanted as long as he would let her go. I was the only one who fought, but he hasn't touched any of us. No matter what our reactions were, he found us lacking in some way, I guess."

Gabriella shook her head. "So, he brought us here because we were a possibility, then he tests us and decides we're not perfect, but then why does he keep us?" She looked up at him for answers.

Jaime hated that he couldn't give them to her—and that hate kept him going. Because at least he still had a conscience. He'd started to worry. "That's where I come in. I've been working my way up to get close to figuring out who he was. When I did that, it was decided I'd stay and get enough information on him that we can arrest and prosecute."

"And you don't have that yet?"

"Not to the extent my superiors would like. Which is why we came up with a plan."

"Let me guess. You can't tell me about the plan."

"Actually, this one I can. A little. You're a gift to me."

She physically recoiled and he could hardly blame her.

"Excuse me?"

"I've slowly become his right-hand man and as I learned about the girls he keeps locked up...I wanted to get close to one of you to figure out how I could get you out. How we could all work together to get you out. So I convinced him that a woman would be better payment than drugs or money. I mean, I get paid, too, bu—"

"Of course you do. I'm sure you get money and a horse and forty acres of land. The payment of a woman is simply pocket change, right?"

"Gabriella."

She began to pace the tiny room, her irritation and anxiety so *recognizable* to him he started to feel the same build in his chest.

"This is insane," she muttered. "This is so impossible. These things don't happen! They don't happen to people in my family. They don't happen to people! This is movie craziness."

"No. It's your life," Jaime returned firmly. He needed her to focus, to get past the panic. "There's one of his compounds that has the most evidence on his whole operation, and it's the only one that I don't know where it's located. So, as I work with him right now, that's what I'm trying to figure out. If you've been watching, paying attention, listening…you might have the answer. But we have to pretend like…"

"Like I'm the gift to you. And you can do whatever you want with me," she said flatly.

"Yes. But the key here is that it's pretend. I'm not going to hurt you. I've done a lot of things that will stick with me for a very long time." He stopped talking for a few seconds so he could regain his composure. He didn't like to think back at some of the chances he'd had to take or some of the people he'd had to hurt. Though he hadn't actively killed anyone, he had no doubt some of the things he'd been in-volved in had led to the death of someone else.

There were a lot of terrible things you could do to a person without killing them.

He had to get hold of himself, so he did. He forced himself to look at Gabriella. She was studying him carefully, as though she could see the turmoil on his face.

To survive, he had to believe this was a very special woman who could see things no one else could. Because if she could see these things and other people could, as well, they would probably both end up dead.

"I know it sounds crazy," she said carefully, "but I know what it's like. I've helped hide drugs that I'm sure have killed people. I've had to dig holes that I think were…so he could bury people. I've had to do terrible things, and sometimes I'm not even sure that I had to. Just that I did."

"No." He took a step toward her and though

he knew he had to be careful so he didn't startle her, he very slowly and gently reached out and took her hand in his. He gave it a slight squeeze.

"We've done what we had to do to survive. In my case, to bring this man to justice. We have to believe that. Above everything else."

She looked down at their joined hands. He had no idea what she saw or what she felt. It had been so long since he'd been able to touch someone in a kind way, in a gentle way, it affected him a bit harder than he'd expected.

Her hand was warm and it felt capable. She squeezed his back as though she could give him some comfort. This woman who'd been abducted from her family for eight years.

When she raised her gaze to his, he felt an odd little jitter deep in his stomach. Something like fear but not exactly. Almost like recognizing something or someone, but that didn't make sense, so he shook it away.

Chapter Four

Gabby looked at her hand, encompassed by a much larger one. She wondered if the small scars across his knuckles were from his under-cover work or if he'd got them before.

What would he have been like before his as-sumed identity?

And what on earth did *that* matter?

She forced her gaze back to him, his dark brown eyes somehow sure and comforting, when nothing in eight years had been *com-forting*. It shouldn't be potent. It was probably part of his training—looking in charge and compassionate.

She'd never been too fond of cops, though that may have been Ricky's influence. Her first serious boyfriend. A poster child for trouble. Gabby had been convinced she could change him, that everyone saw him all wrong. Her parents had been adamant that she could *not* change what was wrong with that boy.

They'd barred him from their house. Insisted Gabby live at home through her coursework at the community college, and had been making noise about her not transferring to get her bachelors.

It had all seemed like the most unjust, unfair fate. They didn't have enough money, they didn't have any trust. The world had seemed cruel, and Ricky had been nice…to her.

She was twenty-eight now and that was the only relationship she'd ever had. A boy, really, and she'd only been a girl.

This man holding her hand was no *boy*, but

she wasn't sure what she was. Except a little off her rocker for having this line of thought.

She cleared her throat and pulled her hand away. "So. What is it you need from me?"

He was quiet for a moment, studying his hand, which he hadn't dropped—it still hovered there in the air between them.

"My main goal is to find the last compound," he finally said, bringing his hand down to his side. "It's the one he's the most secretive about. So much so, I'm not sure he takes any of his employees there."

"I don't know if I can help with that. I did have this theory…" She trailed off. "I wish I had something to write on," she muttered. She searched her room for something…something to illustrate the picture in her head.

She opened one of her drawers and retrieved her brush, pins and ponytail holders, some of the few "extras" The Stallion afforded her. A giddy excitement jumbled through her and maybe she should calm it down.

But this was something. God, *something* to do. Something real. Something that wasn't just pointless fighting but actually working toward a *goal*.

Freedom.

She settled herself at that word. It had come to mean something different in eight years. Or maybe it had come to mean nothing at all.

She shook those oddly uncomfortable thoughts away and looked around for a place to create her makeshift map. "I can't explain it without props," she said, setting a brush on the center of the floor.

"Let's do it on the bed instead of the floor, so if anyone comes in we can…" He rubbed a hand over his unkempt if short beard. "Well, cover it up."

Right. Because to The Stallion she was a *gift*.

No, that was too generous. She was a thing to be traded for services. She shuddered at the thought but…the man kneeled at the bed. The man who hadn't used her as payment but was using her as an informant.

The man whose name she didn't know.

"What should I call you?" she asked suddenly. Because she was working with this man to free—no, not to free anything, but to bring down The Stallion—and she hadn't a clue as to what to call him.

He glanced at her and she must be dreaming the panic she saw in his expression because it disappeared in only a second.

"They call me Rodriguez," he said carefully. "But my name is Jaime A— I…" He shook his head as he focused, as he seemed to push away whatever was plaguing him. "Call me Rodriguez. It's safest."

She knelt next to him, biting back the urge to

repeat *Jaime.* Just to feel what his name would sound like in her mouth.

Silly. "All right, Rodriguez." She placed the brush at the center of the bed. "This is Austin. The bed is Texas. I don't have a clue…" She trailed off, realizing this man would know where they were. He hadn't been blindfolded or hooded. He actually *knew* if they were still in Texas, if they were close to home.

She breathed through the emotion swamping her. "Where are we?" she whispered.

"An hour east of El Paso. Middle of nowhere, basically. Only a few small towns around."

She blinked. El Paso. She'd had theories about where they could be, and El Paso had factored into them, but theories and truths were…

"Take your time," Jaime said gently.

"But we don't have much time, do we?" she returned, staring into compassionate eyes for the first time in eight years. Because as much as all the girls felt sorry for each other, they felt sorry for themselves first and foremost.

Jaime nodded toward the bed. "Technically, I don't know how much time we have. I only know the quicker we figure it out, the less chance he has of hurting people. More people."

She took a deep breath and returned her focus to the bed. "The brush is Austin. I get the feeling that's something like…the center. I don't know if it's a headquarters or…"

"Technically, he lives in Austin. His public persona, anyway."

His public persona. Though it fit everything she knew or had theorized, it was hard to believe The Stallion went about a normal life in Austin and people didn't see something was wrong with the man. Warped and broken beyond comprehension.

"So, we've got his personal center at Austin," Jaime continued for her, taking one of the rubber bands she'd piled next to her. He reached past her, his long, muscular arm brushing against her shoulder. "And this is the compound close to El Paso."

"Right. Right." She picked up another rubber band. "He seems to work by seasons, sort of. I started wondering if he had a place in each direction. If this is west, he has a compound in the north, the south and the east. Unless Austin is his east." She placed rubber bands in general spots that represented each direction, creating a diamond with Austin at the somewhat center.

"He has a compound in the Panhandle. Though I haven't been there, he's talked of it. I've been to the one on the Louisiana border. I didn't think he had women there, but… Now that I've seen this setup, maybe he did and I just didn't know about it."

The idea that there'd been women to help and

he hadn't helped them clearly bothered him, but he kept talking. "But south… He's never mentioned any kind of holdings in the south of Texas." He tapped the lower portion of her bed. "It has to be south."

"It would make sense. The access to drugs, people."

"It would make all the sense in the world, and you, Gabriella, are something of a miracle." He grinned over at her.

"It's…Gabby. Everyone, except *him*, calls me Gabby."

His grin didn't fade so much as morph into something else, something considering or…

The door swung open and the next thing Gabby knew, she was being thrust onto the bed and under a very large man.

JAIME HADN'T HAD a woman underneath him in over two years, and that should not at all be the thought in his head right now. But she was soft underneath him, no matter how strong she was…soft breasts, soft hair.

And a kidnapping victim, jackass.

"Rodriguez. Boss wants you." Layne's cruel mouth was twisted into a smirk, clearly having no compunction about interrupting…well, what this looked like, not so much what it was.

Damn these men and their interruptions. He was getting somewhere, and he didn't mean on top of Gabriella.

Gabby.

He couldn't call her that. Couldn't think of her like that. She was a tool, and a victim. Any slipups and they could both end up dead. He glanced down at her, completely still underneath him, and it was enough of a distraction that he was having trouble deciding how to play things in front of Layne.

She blinked up at him, eyes wide, and though

she wasn't fighting him, he'd scared her. No matter that she understood him, his role here, he didn't think she'd be trusting him any time soon. How could he blame her for that?

Wordlessly he got off Gabby and the bed and straightened his clothes in an effort to make Layne think he was more rumpled than he really was.

"We'll finish this later," he said offhandedly to Gabby, hoping it sounded to Layne like a hideous threat.

Jaime sauntered over to the door, not looking back at Gabby to see what she was doing, though that's desperately what he wanted to do. He grabbed his sunglasses from his pocket and slipped them on his face as he stepped out into the hallway with Layne.

"Awfully clothed, aren't you?" Layne asked.

Jaime closed the door behind him before he answered. "Still trying to knock the fight out of her. Wouldn't want to intimidate her with what's coming." Jaime smirked as if pleased with himself instead of disgusted.

"It's a hell of a lot better when there's still a little fight in them," Layne said, glancing back at Gabby's door as they walked down the hall.

Jaime's body went cold, but he reined in his temper, curling his fingers into fists, his only—and most necessary—reaction.

"Do you think *senor* would be pleased with that world view?" he asked as blandly as he could manage.

Layne's gaze snapped to Jaime and his threat. The man sneered. "Not every idiot believes your Pepe Le Pew act, buddy."

Jaime flashed his most intimidating grin, one devoid of any of the *humanity* he was desperate to believe he still had. "Pepe Le Pew is French, *culo*."

"Whatever," the man said with a disinterested wave. "You know what I mean."

"I know a lot of things about you, *amigo*," Jaime said, enjoying the way the man rolled his eyes at every Spanish word he threw into the conversation.

Layne didn't take the hint. "Maybe you want to pass her around a bit. Boss man's been pretty strict about us getting anything out of these girls but you—"

Jaime stopped and shoved Layne into the wall. What he really wanted to do was punch the man, but he knew that would put his credibility in jeopardy, no matter how much dirt he had on Layne. He wrestled with the impulse, with the beating violence inside him.

No matter what this man might deserve, he was not Jaime's end goal. The end goal was to make this all moot.

So, he held Layne there, against the wall, one

fist bunched in the man's T-shirt to keep him exactly where he wanted him. He stared down at the man with all the menace he felt. "You will not touch what is mine," Jaime threatened, making his intent clear.

"You've already stepped all over what's mine," Layne returned, but Jaime noted he didn't fight back against Jaime's hold—intelligence or strategy, Jaime wasn't sure.

"I ran this show before he brought you in," Layne growled.

"Well, now you answer to me. So, I'd watch your step, *amigo*. I know things about you I don't think The Stallion would particularly care to hear about. A hooker in El Paso, for starters."

Layne blustered, but underneath it the man had paled. This was why Jaime preferred everyone think of him as muscle who could barely understand English. They underestimated him. But Jaime hadn't walked in here blindly. He knew The Stallion's previous head honchos wouldn't take the power share easily. So he'd collected leverage.

Thank God.

"Now, are you ready to keep your disgusting tongue and hands to yourself?" Jaime asked with an almost pleasant smile. "Or do I have to make your life difficult?"

Layne ground his teeth together, a sneer marring his features, but he gave a sharp nod.

"Muy bueno," Jaime said, pretending it was great news as he released the piece of garbage. "Let's proceed, then." He gestured grandly down the hall to the back door.

Layne grumbled something, but Jaime was relieved to see concern and fear on the man's face. He could only hope it would keep the man in line.

They exited the house and Jaime waited

while Layne chained everything up. The late summer sun shimmered in the green of the trees, and if Jaime didn't know what lurked in the shed across the grass, he might have relaxed.

As it was, relaxing wasn't happening any time soon.

Jaime let Layne lead the way to the shed. He preferred to touch as little as possible in that little house of horrors.

Both men stepped in to find The Stallion pacing, hands clutched behind his back, and Wallace looking wary in the far corner.

The Stallion looked up distractedly. "Good. Good. We've gotten news of Herman before Wallace even got anywhere." The man's hands shook as he brought them in front of him in fists, fury stamped across his face. The usual calm calculation in his eyes something darker and more frenzied. "With the Texas Rangers and a hypnotist." The Stallion slammed a fist to the desk that made the creepy-ass dolls on the shelf above shake, their dead lifeless eyes fluttering at the vibration.

Jaime forced himself to look away and stare flatly at his boss. *Fake boss*, he amended.

"Luckily, Mr. Herman doesn't know enough to give them much of a lead, but he certainly represents a loose end." The Stallion took a deep breath, plucking one of the brunette dolls from the shelf. He cradled it like a child.

It took every ounce of Jaime's control and training to keep the horror off his face. Grown men capable of murder cradling a doll was not…comforting in the least.

"I've sent a team to get rid of Herman. Scare the hypnotist. I don't think I want to extinguish her yet. She might be valuable. But I want her *scared*." He squeezed the doll so tight it was a wonder one of its plastic limbs didn't break off.

"There we are, pretty girl," The Stallion cooed, resettling the doll on the shelf and brushing a hand over its fake hair.

Jaime shuddered and looked away.

"Until this mess is taken care of, you are all on lockdown. No one is leaving the premises until Herman is taken care of."

"Then, boss?" Layne asked a little too hopefully.

The Stallion smiled pleasantly. "And then we'll decide what to do about the hypnotist."

Lockdown and death threats. Jaime tried to breathe through the urgency, the failure, the impossibility of saving this man's life.

He'd try. Somehow, he'd try. But he had the sinking suspicion Herman was already gone.

Chapter Five

Gabby couldn't sleep. It wasn't an uncommon affliction. Even in the past two years, exercising herself to exhaustion, giving up on things ever being different, avoiding figuring out the pieces of The Stallion puzzle, insomnia still plagued her.

Because no matter how she tried to accept her lot in life, she'd always known this wasn't *home*.

But what *would* be home? Her father was dead. Her sister would be an adult woman with a life of her own. Would Mom and Grandma still live in the little house on East Avenue or would they have moved?

Did they assume she was dead? Would they have kept all her things or gotten rid of them? The blue teddy bear Daddy had given her on her sixth birthday. The bulletin board of pictures of friends and Ricky and her and Nattie.

Her heart absolutely ached at the thought of her sister. Two years apart, they hadn't always gotten along, but they had been friends. Sisters. They'd shared things, laughed together, cried together, fought together.

Tears pricked Gabby's eyes. She hadn't had this kind of sad nostalgia swamp her in years, because it led nowhere good. She couldn't change her circumstances. She was stuck in this prison and there was no way out.

Except maybe Jaime.

That was not an acceptable thought. She could work with him to take down The Stallion, and she would, but actually thinking she could get out of there was… It was another thing altogether.

She froze completely at the telltale if faint sound of her door opening. And then closing. She closed her hands into fists, ready to fight. She couldn't drown that reaction out of herself, no matter how often she wondered if giving in was simply easier.

"Gabby."

A hushed whisper, but even if she didn't re-member people's voices so easily, she would have known it was Jaime—*Rodriguez*—from a man calling her Gabby.

Gabby. She swallowed against all of the fuzzy feelings inside her. Home and Gabby and what did either even mean anymore. She didn't have a home. The Gabby she'd been was dead.

It didn't matter. Taking The Stallion down

was the only thing that mattered. She sat up in the dark, watched Jaime's shadow get closer.

The initial fear hadn't totally subsided. She wasn't *afraid* of him per se or, maybe more accurately, she wasn't afraid he would harm her. But that didn't mean there weren't other things to be afraid of.

She had sat up on the bed, but he still loomed over her from his standing position. She banked the edgy nerves fluttering inside her chest.

He kneeled, much like he had earlier today when they'd been putting together her map. Except she was on the bed instead of her make-shift markers.

"Do you have any more ideas about the locations? Aside from directions?" he asked, everything about him sounding grave and…tired.

"I have a few theories. Do we…do we need to go over all that tonight?"

"I'm sorry. You were sleeping."

"Well, no." She had the oddest urge to offer her hand to him. He'd taken her hand earlier today and there had been something... "Is something wrong?"

He laughed, caustic and bitter, and she didn't know this man. He could be lying to her. He could be anyone. Then there was her, cut off from normal human contact for *eight* years. The only place she had to practice any kind of compassion or reading of people was with the other girls, and she'd been keeping her distance lately.

So she was probably way off base to think something was wrong, to feel like he was off somehow.

But he stood, pacing away from the bed, a dark, agitated shadow. "It doesn't get any easier to know someone's going to die. I tried..." He shook his head grimly. "We should focus on what we can do."

"You tried what?" Gabby asked, undeterred.

"I tried to get a message to the Rangers, but…" He kneeled again and she couldn't see him in the dark, found it odd she wanted to.

"But?"

"I think it was too late."

Gabby inhaled sharply. Whether she knew him or not, whether she'd lost all ability to gauge people's emotions, she could all but *feel* his guilt and regret as though it were her own.

She didn't know what the answer to that was…what he might have endured in pretending to be the kind of man who worked for The Stallion. Gabby couldn't begin to imagine… Though she'd ostensibly worked for the man, she'd never had to pretend she liked it.

"If we're an hour west of El Paso, I would imagine each spot would be likely the same distance from the city in its sector," she said, because the only answer she knew was bringing The Stallion down.

It couldn't bring dead people back, including herself, but it could stop the spread. They had to stop the spread.

She kept going when he said nothing. "He's very methodical. Things are the same. He stays here the same weeks every year. He eats the same things, does the same things. I would imagine whatever other places he has are like this one. Possibly identical."

In the dark she couldn't see what Jaime's face might be reflecting and he was completely and utterly still.

"Jaime…"

"Rodriguez. We have to…we can't be too complacent. There's too much at stake. I am Rodriguez."

"Okay," she returned, and she supposed he was right, no matter how much she preferred to call him something—anything—other than what The Stallion called him.

"But you're right. The eastern compound was around an hour west of Houston. I wonder… He is methodical, you're right about that. I wonder if the mileage would be exactly the same."

"It wouldn't shock me."

"Have you seen the dolls?"

Gabby could only blink in Jaime's shadow's direction. "Dolls?"

"He has a shelf of dolls in his office. They sit in a row. I'd always thought they were creepy, but today…" Jaime laughed again, this one wasn't quite as bitter as the one before, but it certainly wasn't true humor. "You should get some rest. I didn't mean to interrupt you. We can talk in the morning." He got to his feet.

She didn't analyze why she bolted off the bed to follow him. Even if she gave herself the brain time to do it, she wouldn't have come up with an answer.

He was a lifeline. To what, she didn't know. She didn't have a life—not one here, not one to go back to.

"I wasn't sleeping." She scurried between him and the room's only exit. "What about the dolls?"

He was standing awfully close in his attempt to leave, but he neither reached around her for the door nor pushed her out of the way. He simply stood there, an oppressive, looming shadow.

Gabby didn't know what possessed her, why she thought in a million years it was appropriate to reach out and touch a man she'd only met today. But what did it *matter*? She'd been here eight years and worrying about normal or appropriate had left the building a long time ago.

So she placed her palm on his chest, hard

and hot even through the cotton of his T-shirt. Such a strange sensation to touch someone in neither fight nor comfort. Just gentle and…a connection.

"Tell me about the dolls," she said in the same tone she used with the girls when she wanted them to listen and stop whining. "Get it off your chest."

HIS CHEST. WHERE Gabby's hand was currently touching him between the vee of straps that kept his weapons at hand. Gently, very nearly *comfortingly*, her hand rested in the center of all that violent potential.

Jaime was not in a world where that had happened for years. His mother had hugged him hard and long that last meal before he'd gone undercover, and that had been it. Two years, three months and twenty-one days ago.

He had known what he was getting himself

into and yet he hadn't. There had been no way to anticipate the toll it would take, the length of time and how far he'd gotten.

That meant bringing The Stallion to justice was really the only thing that could matter, not a woman's hand on his chest.

And yet he allowed himself the briefest moment of putting his hand over hers. He allowed himself a second of absorbing the warmth, the proof of beating life and humanity, before he peeled her hand off his chest.

"He cradled the doll like a baby. Talked to it. Damn creepiest thing I've ever seen—and I've seen some things." He said it all flippantly, trying to imbue some humor into the statement, but it felt good to get it out.

The image haunted him. A grown man. A doll. The threat on a man who would most certainly be dead even if Jaime's secret message to his FBI superiors made it through.

Dead. Herman, a man he'd never met and knew next to nothing about, was dead. Because he hadn't been able to stop it.

"Dolls." Gabby seemed to ponder this, and though her hand was no longer on his chest, she still stood between him and the door, far too close for anyone's good.

"If there are identical dolls in every compound, I'll never be able to sleep again after this is all over."

Even in the dark he could see her head cock, could *feel* her gaze on him. "Do you think of after?"

"Sometimes," he offered truthfully, though the truth was the last thing they should be discussing. "Sometimes I have to or I'm afraid I'll forget it isn't real."

"I stopped believing 'after' could be real," she whispered, heavy and weighted in the dark room of a deranged man's hideout.

He wanted to touch her again. Cradle her small but competent hand in his larger one against his chest. He wanted to make her a million promises he couldn't keep about *after*.

"I…I can't think about after, but I can think about ending him. If we're an hour west of El Paso, give or take, and the western compound is an hour west of Houston, then what would the southern compound be? San Antonio?"

"If we're going from the supposition it's the closest guarded one because it's closest to the border, I think it'd be farther south."

"Yes." She made some movement, though he couldn't make it out in the dark. Likely they could turn on the lights and no one would think anything of it, she had been a gift to him, after all, but he found as long as she didn't turn on the lights, he didn't want to, either.

There was something comforting about the dark. About this woman he didn't know. About the ability to say that a man's life wasn't saved probably because of him. Because who else could he express that remorse to? No one here. No one in his undercover life.

He finally realized she had moved around him. She wasn't exactly pacing, but neither was she still in the pitch-black room.

He couldn't begin to imagine how she'd done it. This darkness. This uncertainty. For eight years she had been at someone else's mercy. As much as he sometimes felt like he was at someone else's mercy, it was voluntary. It was for a higher purpose. If he really wanted to, if he didn't care about bringing The Stallion down, he could walk away from all this.

But she was here and said she couldn't even think about after. Instead she lived and fought and puzzled things together in her head. Remembered things no one would expect her to.

She was the key to this investigation. Because she'd been that strong.

"Loredo, maybe?" she offered.

"It's possible," Jaime returned, reminding himself to focus on the task at hand rather than this woman. "Doesn't quite match the pattern of being close to bigger cities like Houston and El Paso."

"True, and he does like his patterns." She was quiet for a minute. "But what about the northern compound? There isn't anything up there that matches Houston or El Paso, either. Maybe whatever town in the south it's near matches whatever town is north."

"I haven't been to the northern one, so I don't know for sure, but one would assume Amarillo. Based on what I know."

"Laredo and Amarillo would be similar. Was the place west of Houston similar to this?"

It was something Jaime hadn't given much

thought to, but now that she mentioned it… "I never went in the house, but there was one. It didn't look the same from the outside, but it's very possible that the layout inside was exactly the same."

"If you didn't go in the house, where did you go there?"

It confirmed Jaime's suspicion that the girls didn't know anything about the outside world around them. "He has a shed for an office outside."

"It must be in the back. He had us dig holes in the front."

It shouldn't shock him The Stallion used the women he kidnapped for manual labor, and yet the thought of Gabby digging shallow graves for that man settled all wrong in his gut. "Did you ever see…?"

"We just dug the holes and were ushered back inside," she replied, her tone flat. Though she had brought it up yesterday when they'd first met, so clearly it bugged her. "It's the only time I've been out…" She shook her head. "The office shed. Is the one here the same as the one in the west?"

He wanted to tell her she'd make a good cop—focusing on the facts and details over emotions—but that spoke of an after she couldn't bring herself to consider. So he answered her question instead.

"The one he has here is a little bit more involved than the one he had there. And no dolls."

"The doll thing really bothers you, huh?"

"Hey, you watch a grown man cradle and coo at a doll the way a normal person would an infant and tell me you wouldn't be haunted for life."

Though it was dark and Jaime had no idea if his instincts were accurate without seeing her expression, he thought maybe she was teasing him. An attempt at lightening things a little. He appreciated that, even if it was a figment of his imagination.

"As long as I'm on lockdown, I can't share any of this information with my superiors. It would be too dangerous and too risky, and I've already risked enough by trying to warn them about…" He trailed off, that inevitable, heavy guilt choking out the words.

"If the man ends up dead, it has nothing to do with you," Gabby said firmly.

"It's hardly nothing. I knew. And I didn't stop it."

"Because you're here to bring down The Stallion. Doing that is going to save more men than saving one man. Maybe I wouldn't have thought about it that way years ago, but… You begin to learn that you can't save everyone, and that some things happen whether it's *fair* or not. I hate the word *fair*. Nothing is fair."

That was not something he could even begin to argue with a woman who'd been kidnapped eight years ago.

"Do you know who this man was?" she demanded in the inky dark.

"He delivered messages for The Stallion."

"Then I don't feel sorry for him at all."

"You don't?" he asked, surprised at her vehemence for a man she didn't know.

"No. He worked for that man, and I don't care who you are or how convincing he is in his real life, if you work for that man, you deserve whatever you get."

She said it flatly, with certainty, and there was a part of him that wanted to argue with her. Because he knew things like this could make you hard. Rightfully so, even. She deserved her anger and hatred and her uncompromising views.

But he could not adopt them as his own. He was afraid if he did that he would never find his way out of this. That he would become Rodriguez for life and forget who Jaime Alessandro was. It was his biggest fear.

He felt sorry for Gabby, but it made him all the more determined to make sure she got out. He would make sure she had a chance to find her compassion again.

"Until I can get more intel to my superiors, the next step is to keep gathering as much information as we can. The more I can give them when the time comes, the better chance we have of ending this once and for all."

"End." She laughed, an odd sound, neither bitter nor humorous. Just kind of a noise. "I'm not sure I know what that word means anymore."

"I'll teach you." That was a foolish thing to say, and yet he would. He would find a way to show her what endings meant. And what new beginnings could be about.

Because if he could show her, then he could believe he could show himself.

Chapter Six

Gabby was tired and bleary-eyed the next day. Jaime had stayed in her room for most of the night and they had talked about The Stallion, sure, but as the night had worn on, they'd started to veer toward things they remembered about their former lives.

She'd kept telling herself to stop, not to tell yet another story about Natalie or not to listen to another about the birthday dinners his mother used to make him. And yet remembering her family and the woman she'd been years ago—which had never been tempting to her in all these years—had been more than just tempting in a dark room with Jaime.

She should think of him as nothing but Rodriguez. She shouldn't be forming some odd friendship with a man whose only job was to bring down The Stallion. Knowing those things seemed to disappear when she was actually in a room with him.

He was fascinating and kind. She missed kindness. In a way she hadn't been able to articulate in the past eight years. The other kidnapped girls were mostly nice. Alyssa was a little hard, but Gabby had spent many a night holding Jasmine or Tabitha as they cried. She had reassured them they wouldn't be hurt and hoped she wasn't lying. She had given them all kindness and compassion, but there was something about being the first—the older member, so to speak—that meant none of the girls offered the same to her.

Gabby was the mother figure. The martyr to them. Everyone thought she was strong and fine and somehow surviving this. But she wasn't. She was broken.

Jaime saw the victim in her, though. It should be awful, demoralizing, and yet it was the most comforted she'd felt in eight years.

But it would weaken her. It *was* weakening her. There was this war in her brain and her heart whether that weakening mattered.

Maybe she should be weak. Maybe she should lean completely on this strange angel of a man and let him take care of everything. If it all worked out in the end and The Stallion was brought down, and she was free—

She wasn't going to go that far. She'd save thinking about freedom for after.

So she sat at the kitchen table with Jasmine, Tabitha and Alyssa eating breakfast and wondering what Jaime would be up to this morning. Would he be as exhausted as she was? Would he be thinking of her?

Foolish girl. But it nearly made her smile—to feel foolish and stupid. It was somehow a comfort to know she could be something normal. Stupid felt deliciously normal.

At Jasmine's sharply inhaled gasp, Gabby glanced up from her microwaved oatmeal. All the girls were looking wide-eyed at the entrance to the hallway.

Jaime stood there in his dedicated black, weapons strapped against his chest. Those sunglasses on his face. Gabby wondered if there was a purpose to always wearing them. So no one could see the kindness in his eyes. Because even in the dark she had to think that kindness would radiate off a man like him.

Since the girls seemed scared into silence, she nodded toward him. "Rodriguez."

"You know him?" Jasmine squeaked under her breath.

"He's The Stallion's new right-hand man." She looked back at Jaime and tried to work on the sarcastic sneer she sent most of the guards. "Right?"

Jaime's lips quirked and she could almost believe it was in pride, but she saw the disgust lingering underneath it.

Was she the only one who saw that? Based on the way Jasmine scooted closer to her, as though Gabby could protect her from the man, Gabby wondered.

"Senorita."

It took everything in her not to roll her eyes at him and smile at that exaggerated accent.

"You're wanted privately, Gabriella," he said with enough menace she should have been scared. She didn't think the little fissure of nerves that went through her was *fear*.

"But, please, finish your *desayuno*. I am nothing if not gracious with my time."

Gabby began to push her chair back, the crappy packet oatmeal completely forgotten. But Jasmine's fingers curled around her arm and held on tight.

"Don't go, Gabby. Fight."

Gabby looked down at Jasmine, surprised that none of the women seemed to see the lack of threat underneath Jaime's act. But then, they didn't know what she knew. Maybe that made all the difference.

"It's all right. When have I ever not been able to handle myself?" She smiled reassuringly at… Sometimes she thought of the girls as her friends. Sometimes as her charges. And sometimes simply people she didn't really know. She didn't know what she felt today. But she patted Jasmine's arm before peeling the woman's fingers off her wrist. "I'll be back for lunch."

"Don't make promises you can't keep, *senorita*."

She shot Jaime a glare she didn't have to fake. He didn't have to make these women more scared. They already did that themselves.

She walked over to where Jaime stood in the entrance to the hallway. He made a grand gesture with his arm. "After you, Gabriella."

Again she had to fight to mask her face from amusement. He should go into acting once this was all over. The stage where his over-the-top antics might be appreciated.

As she began to walk down the corridor to her room, Jaime's hand clamped on her shoulder. Hot and hard and tight. She didn't have to feign the shiver or the wild worry that shot through her.

It wasn't comfortable that he could turn himself on and off so easily. It wasn't comfortable that, though she was intrigued by the man and convinced of his kindness, she didn't know him at all. Anything he'd told her so far could be lies.

When he acted like this other man, she could remember she shouldn't trust him. She couldn't believe everything he said. He could be as big a liar as The Stallion, and just as dangerous.

But they walked to her room with his hand clamped on her shoulder and somehow in the short walk it became something of a comfort. A calming presence of strength. She missed someone else having strength. True courage. Not the strength The Stallion or his guards exerted. Not that physical, brute force.

No, Jaime was full of certainty. Confidence. He was full of righteous goodness and she wanted to follow that anywhere it would lead.

She wanted to believe in righteous goodness again. That it was possible. That it could save her.

And what will happen after you're saved?

Jaime closed the door behind them, taking off his sunglasses and sliding them into his pocket. Immediately his entire demeanor changed. How did he do it? She opened her mouth to ask him but he seemed suddenly rushed.

"We don't have much time. There's a meeting in ten minutes and Layne will be sent to fetch me. I need…when he comes…"

She cocked her head because he didn't finish his sentence. He studied her and then he swallowed, almost nervously. "I'll have to, uh, do what I did the other day."

"The other day?"

"I'll try not to rip your shirt, but I'm going to need to…er, well, grab you."

"Oh." She let out a shaky breath, the white-hot fear of that moment revisiting her briefly. "Right. Well, okay. But, uh, you know, not ripping my clothes would be preferred, if only because I don't have many."

His lips almost curved, but mostly something heavily weighted his mouth and him. She supposed he could play the part of Rodriguez easily enough in front of whoever walked through, but demonstrating the physical force expected of him? No. She couldn't imagine Jaime ever getting comfortable with that.

Maybe she was wrong. Maybe she was making everything up. Maybe he enjoyed scaring women and she was stupidly coping by turning him into a hero.

If a hero hadn't saved her in the past eight years, why would she think one would now?

"What do you know about his schedule? You said something about him staying certain times in certain places. Is he usually here, at this location, at this time?"

Gabby filtered through her memories. The

ways she used to count days. Her many theories about The Stallion's yearly travel.

"Yes. He'd usually be here, but getting ready to leave." She tried to work out the days that would be left, but she'd stopped paying such close attention to the days and—

The thought hit her abruptly—a sharp blow to the chest as she met his intense brown gaze. "You know what day it is." She'd meant that to be a question, not the shaky accusation it had turned into.

He blinked down at her. Something in his face softened and then shuttered blank. "August 23, 2017."

She did the math in her head, trying to get through the shaky feeling of knowing what day it was. What actual day. For so long she'd known, but in the past two years she'd let it slide to seasons at most.

It was 2017. She'd been here for the entirety of the 2010s.

"Gabby." He touched her shoulder again, not the hard clamp of a guiding hand but a gentle laying of his palm to the slope of her arm. It was weird not to flinch. Weird not to want to. She wanted to lean into the strong presence. To the way he seemed to have everything under control…even when he didn't.

"August twenty-third. I would say usually he leaves for the southern compound on the twenty-sixth. I think. Around there. Never quite at the end of the month, but close."

Jaime smiled down at her, clearly pleased with the information.

When was the last time she'd seen a smile that wasn't sarcastic? When had anyone tried to smile at her reassuringly in eight long years? It hadn't happened.

She quashed the emotional upheaval inside

her. Or, at least, she tried. It must've showed on her face, though, because he moved his hand up to her cheek, a rough, calloused warmth against her skin.

She knew he wanted to fix this for her. To promise her safety. But she didn't want to hear it. Promises… No, she wanted nothing to do with those.

JAIME WAS LOSING track of time and it wouldn't do. But she looked so sad. So completely overwhelmed by the weight of her existence here. He wanted to do something, anything, to comfort her. To take the tears in her eyes away, to take the despair on her face and stamp it out. He wanted to promise her safety and hope and a new life.

But he could promise none of those things. This was dangerous business, and they could easily end up dead. Both of them.

No matter that he would do everything in his power to not let that happen, it didn't mean it wasn't possible. It would be worse to promise something he couldn't deliver than to fail his mission.

"That means we'll have to wait about three more days. If he has me stay here while he goes to the southern compound, it gives me the opportunity to get this new information to my superiors. If he wants me to go with him, then I'll know where it is. Either way, we win."

"We may win the battle but not the war," she stated simply, resolutely. He wondered if she was just a little too afraid of getting hopes up herself.

He brushed his thumb down her cheek, even though it was the last thing he should've done. But though she was probably more gaunt than she would have been had she been living her actual life, though she was pale when the rich olive of her complexion should be sun-kissed, she was soft. And something special.

Her eyebrows drew together, but she wasn't looking at him. She was looking at the door and she mouthed something to him, but he couldn't catch what it was. She didn't hesitate. She grabbed him by the shoulders and pulled him close, her big brown eyes wide but determined. She mouthed the words again and this time he thought he caught them.

The door. Someone was at the door. Behind the door. That meant there was only one thing he could do. He choked back his complicated emotions and dropped his mouth to her ear.

"I'm going to kiss you. It won't be nice. The minute the door opens, shove me away with everything you've got. Understand?"

Her eyes were still wide, her hands on his shoulders. As if she trusted him.

She gave a nod and all he could do was say

a little prayer that this would not be…complicated. But if someone was listening at the door, he had to prove he was Rodriguez and nothing more. That meant not being nice. That meant taking what he wanted whether it was what she wanted. And then, somehow, not getting lost in that. Humanity. His calling card. To keep his humanity.

But first… First he had to be Rodriguez. That meant he could not gently lower his mouth to hers. He had to take. He had to plunder.

And he had to stop talking to himself about it and do it.

He slid his arm around her waist and pulled her to him roughly. It was both regret and something far darker he didn't want to analyze that twined through him. He crushed his mouth to hers if only to stop his brain from moving in this hideous circle.

He focused on the fact that it wasn't supposed to be nice or easy. It was supposed to scare and intimidate. If she trembled, he was only doing his job. He was proving to everyone that he was Rodriguez—awful and mean, a broken excuse for a human being.

He thrust his tongue into her mouth and tried not to commit her taste to memory. But when was the last time he'd tasted a woman? Sweet and hot. Uncertain, and yet, brave with it. She let his tongue explore her mouth and she did not fight him.

He scraped his teeth along her plump bottom lip and fought to remember who he really was. Not this man, but a man with a badge. A protector. A believer in law and order.

Gabby's fingers tensed on his shoulders and then relaxed. She did something that felt like a sigh against his mouth, and then he was being pushed violently back and away from sweet perfection.

He allowed himself two steps from the shove before stopping. He did everything to ignore the way his body trembled. Ignored the desperate erection pressing against his jeans. Ignored the inappropriate desire running through his blood. It was wrong and it was cruel but surely his body's natural reaction to that sort of thing after such a long absence.

Or so he told himself.

He didn't look at Gabby because it would surely unman him completely. Instead he turned to face the interruption with a sneer on his mouth.

Layne didn't need to know the hatred in his expression was for himself, not the interruption.

"You have the worst timing, *amigo*," he said, trying to eradicate the affectedness from his voice. "I grow weary of it."

Layne snorted. "You knew I was coming to

fetch you at one. And here you are, yet again, clothed and being pushed around by a woman. Starting to question your strength, Rodriguez."

"Question all you want. Then test me. I'd love you to."

Layne merely crossed his hands over his chest. "Boss wants us now."

"*Sí.*" Jaime strode to the door, making sure never to look back at Gabby. The only reason Jaime paused in the hallway instead of going straight to The Stallion was to ensure Layne left Gabby's room without saying a damn thing. Because if that man said something to her...

Jaime balled his hands into fists. He had to get his temper under control. He wasn't pissed off at Layne. The man had done exactly what he was supposed to.

Jaime was pissed at himself.

Much like the afternoon before, Jaime let

Layne lead him down the hall and outside. When they entered the shed this time, The Stallion's demeanor was calm rather than the unhinged anger of yesterday. He was sitting at his desk all but smiling.

"You're late. I suggest you get that kind of impulse under control. I demand timeliness in all things, gentlemen."

"*Sí, senor.*"

"Now that that's been taken care of, we have our next target."

"The hypnotist?" Wallace asked from the corner.

"Yes, but not just her. A Texas Ranger has taken it upon himself to protect this young woman. I sent two men to follow them and to bring her to me." The Stallion reclined in his chair, his smile widening.

"What about the Ranger?" Jaime asked.

"He's of no use to us. I want her," The Stallion said with a sneer. "I hate when law enforcement try to get in my way. Bunch of useless pigs. We'll get rid of him and take the girl. The girl is *very* important." The Stallion's empty blue eyes zeroed in on Jaime. "There is a message I want you to deliver to our Gabriella, Rodriguez."

Jaime tried to maintain a blank expression, but it was hard with the addition of Gabby into the conversation. That should be a warning in it of itself that he was letting himself get too wrapped up in this whole thing.

"The hypnotist has quite the interesting connection to our oldest guest."

"Connection?" Jaime repeated, hoping he covered the demand with enough confusion in his tone to make The Stallion think it was a language barrier issue.

"Natalie Torres is our hypnotist. Whatever Herman told her and this Ranger, I want to know it. But more, I want the girl." The Stallion turned his computer screen to face Layne and Jaime. "The resemblance. Do you see it?"

Jaime schooled himself into complete indifference. *"Sí."* The woman in the picture was more slight of build than Gabby and she had a softer chin and a sharper nose. But she had the same mass of curly black hair. The same big brown eyes.

"Tell our Gabriella her sister will be joining us soon. Make sure you mention how close she was to being the perfect woman. Perhaps her sister will fit the role she could not." The Stallion leaned back in his chair, smiling a self-satisfied smirk.

Jaime tried to match it, afraid it only looked like a scowl. But if he failed, The Stallion was too happy with himself to notice.

Chapter Seven

Gabby knew it was beyond foolish to wait in the dark and hope Jaime would come to her again. She'd answered the questions he'd needed answered and he probably had hench-man things to do.

Besides, she didn't really want to see him. Not after that kiss, which was hardly fair to call a kiss since it wasn't real. Like her life. It was a shallow approximation of something else. No matter how his mouth on hers had rioted through her like some sort of miracle.

She was clearly delirious or crazy. Maybe it

was some sort of rescue-fantasy type thing that all kidnap victims succumbed to. She didn't know, and it wouldn't matter. Because it had all been fake. It had been a show.

Layne was… Gabby didn't know if "suspicious" was the right word, but he clearly didn't like Jaime and that was going to be dangerous. Because he would be watching him and making sure that whatever moves he made matched up with the man he was supposed to be. Making enemies as an undercover agent had to be incredibly dangerous and Layne was clearly Jaime's enemy.

Maybe she should think up something that could help Jaime in that regard. Surely there had to be something she'd witnessed or put together that would make all of this moot. Something he could tell his superiors that would make sure they felt like they had enough to prosecute.

Maybe if she told him the exact location of the holes she'd had to dig two summers ago, Jaime could find out what was buried there. Maybe that would be enough. Surely a dead body or two would be something.

If they could get through the next two days, and The Stallion left, surely Jaime could do a little figurative and literal digging.

She could make a map, like the one they'd made when trying to figure out the locations of the other compounds. But it would be difficult without paper. It would be difficult without being outside and working through landmarks. Maybe Jaime could sneak her out once The Stallion was gone.

She very nearly laughed at herself. Yes, after eight years she was going to sneak outside and bring The Stallion down with an undercover FBI agent. That was about as plausible as getting kidnapped, she supposed. But then what?

She'd go back to her life? Eight years missing and she'd just waltz back into her old life? Twenty-eight with eight years of absolutely no education or work experience. Eight years without a *life*.

Maybe she could add digging shallow graves to her résumé. *Excellent seamstress. Know just where to hide the drugs.*

This was such stupidity. Why was she even going down this road? The future had never held any appeal, and it still didn't. Jaime was here to do a job, and she'd do whatever he needed, but she certainly wasn't going to allow fantasies about escaping. About helping him or saving him from his gruesome undercover work.

The door opened and Gabby's heart jumped to her throat. Not as it had the night before. That night, she'd been scared. This night she was anything but.

She scrambled into a sitting position. But instead of staying in the dark, or saying her name, Jaime turned on the light. She blinked against the sudden brightness.

"I apologize," he said, his tone strangely bland, maybe a little tense. "I should've warned you."

"It's all right," she replied carefully, trying to read the blank expression on his face. He was tense and not like she'd ever seen him before. Because this wasn't his Rodriguez acting, and it wasn't exactly the honest and competent Jaime, either.

"Is everything all right?" she asked after he stood there in silence for ticking seconds.

"I want you to know that it will be. But there is some uncomfortable information I have to share with you."

Her heart sank, hard and sharp. She realized who this Jaime was. FBI Agent Jaime. A little aloof, delivering bad news. Probably how he delivered the news to a family that someone was dead.

"Uncomfortable?" she repeated, because surely if another one of her family members was dead it would be more than *uncomfortable*.

"If I could spare you this, I would," he said, taking a step toward her, some of his natural-born compassion leaking through. "But I have to do what The Stallion asks right now."

A shiver of fear took hold of her, with deep awful claws, and she pressed herself into the corner of where her bed met the wall.

But this was Jaime, and he wasn't going to hurt her just because The Stallion told him to. She wanted to believe that. But for a moment she wondered if something in her would have to be sacrificed to take The Stallion down.

"It's just a message, Gabby," he said softly. "I won't hurt you. I promise. No matter what."

Part of her wanted to cry. Over the fact he could see through her so easily. The fact she could feel guilty over making him think that she thought he was going to hurt her. She wanted to cry at the unfairness of it all, and that was just…so seven years ago.

She straightened with a deep breath and fixed him with her most competent I-can-handle-anything expression. "Just tell me. Say it outright."

"The Stallion is after your sister."

Gabby thought she couldn't be surprised at what horrors The Stallion could do. After all, he'd gleefully informed her of her father's heart attack. Made it very clear she had been the cause. She knew The Stallion killed, and extorted, and hurt people.

He was after her sister. Her Nattie. There was

no way to be calm in the face of it. She jumped off the bed and reached for Jaime.

"He doesn't have her," he said calmly. So damn calm. "And she's with a Texas Ranger who will do everything in his power to protect her—that, I know for sure."

"But he's after her. He's after *her*. Purposefully. Why? Why?"

Jaime took her by the shoulders, looking her directly in the eye. She could see all of that compassion and all of the right he wanted to do. No matter how she told herself not to believe in it. No matter how she told herself it was a figment of her imagination and that he couldn't really be good, she felt it. She *believed* it and knew it. No amount of reason seemed to change the fact that she trusted him.

"She has something to do with the dead messenger. I don't know the whole story yet, but I think she knows something. She's a hypnotist working with the Rangers, and if she's with the police… This could be… It could be a positive development. I know it doesn't feel like that, but this could be a positive."

"Is she…is she looking for me?" Gabby asked, ashamed that her voice wavered. But Nattie, a hypnotist, working with the Rangers? It didn't make sense. And Gabby was afraid of whatever the answer would be. If Natalie was looking for her, Nat had wasted eight years of her life. If she wasn't and this was some cosmic coincidence…

Jaime's strong hands squeezed her shoulders. Comforting. Strong. "I don't know. I don't know why your sister was in that interrogation room with The Stallion's messenger. I don't know why…" He shook his head, regret and frustration in the movement. "I wish I knew more, but I don't. But The Stallion wants you to know he's after your sister because he wants to break you."

Maybe if it had been her and The Stallion alone delivering his message, it would have succeeded in breaking her. But something about having Jaime there, something about feeling his strength and his certainty that this could work out…

"He won't break me," Gabby said firmly.

Jaime's mouth curved, one of those kind smiles that tried to comfort her. It made her feel as though…as though there was hope. That was dangerous. Hope was such a dangerous thing here.

"You're an incredibly brave woman," Jaime said, giving her shoulders yet another squeeze.

The compliment warmed her far too much. Much more so than when the girls gave it to her. Then it felt like a weight, a responsibility, but when Jaime said it, it sounded like an *asset*.

"It's not exactly brave to survive a kidnapping. You don't get much of a choice." No, choice was not something she had any of.

"There is always a choice. And the ones you've made have made this possible, Gabby. The things you remember, the theories you've come up with… You're making this all the more possible. I know you don't believe in endings, or maybe you can't see the possibility of them, but I am going to end this. One way or another, we will end him."

We. It was that final straw, a thing she couldn't fight. To be a "we" after so long of feeling like an I. Like the only one who could do something or be something or fight something.

"I believe you," she whispered. *Too much.* She shouldn't feel it, and she shouldn't say it. She should feel none of the things washing through her at the way his face changed over her saying she believed him.

She shouldn't want to kiss this man she'd known for two days. She shouldn't want to feel what it would be like for him to kiss her for real. Without weapons and fake identities between them.

But there was something kind of beautiful about being a kidnap victim in this case. That she had no life to ruin, no self to endanger. Nothing to lose, really. There was only her.

What choices did she have? Jaime thought she had a choice, but he was wrong. She was nothing here. A ghost at best. What she did or didn't do didn't truly matter.

Even now, with The Stallion after Natalie, there was nothing she could do except hope and pray the Texas Ranger with her was a smart man, and a good man, and would protect

Natalie the way Jaime was protecting Gabby right now.

Because no matter that he shouldn't, she knew that was the decision he'd made. He would protect her above himself.

Tentatively she touched her fingertips to the vee of his chest between the straps of guns. She could feel underneath her fingertips the heavy beating of his heart. A little fast, as though he had the same kinds of swirling emotions inside him that she had inside her. She glanced up at him through her lashes, trying to read the expression on his face. A face she'd memorized. A face she thought she would always remember now.

There was enough of a height difference that she would have to pull him down to meet her mouth.

It was such an absurd thought, the idea of wrapping her arms around his neck and pulling his lush mouth to hers. She smiled a little at the insanity of her brain. And he smiled back.

"Thank you for that," he said.

She had lost the thread of the conversation and had no idea what he was thanking her for. All she could think about was the fact he was stepping away from her. Letting her shoulders go and making enough distance that her fingers fell from his chest.

"I should let you sleep," he said, backing slowly away and toward the door.

Gabby should leave it at that. She should let him go and she should sleep. But instead she shook her head.

"Please don't go. Stay."

IT WAS WRONG. It would be wrong to stay. It would be wrong to let her touch him. It would be wrong to let her belief in him change anything. It didn't matter. All that mattered was doing his duty. His duty included protecting her, not…

"There are things I could tell you," Gabby offered, for the first time in all their minutes together seeming nervous without fear behind it. "More things to help with making sure we can end this."

It didn't escape him the way she halted over the word "end." Like she still didn't quite believe a life outside these walls could exist, but she was trying to believe in one. For him? For herself? He had no idea.

He only knew that everything he should do was tangled up in things he shouldn't. Right and wrong didn't always make sense anymore, and it would take nothing at all for him to lose sight of the fact that anything more than a business partnership with her was a gross dereliction of duty. It was taking advantage of a woman who had already been taken so much advantage of.

But she wanted him to stay. She wanted him to stay. Not the other way around.

"I was just thinking before you got here that if I could tell you where the holes were that we dug two years ago, you might be able to connect it all together. If The Stallion does go in a few days, you'd be able to dig it up or something, and… Maybe that would be… Surely finding a body would be enough. Your superiors would want to press charges at that point, wouldn't they?"

The way she cavalierly talked about digging holes for bodies scraped him raw. It had always been hard to accept that there were people in the world who could hurt other people in such cruel and unusual ways. He'd always had a hard time reconciling the world as he wanted it—with law and order and good people—to the world that was with people who broke those laws and that order and had no good intentions whatsoever.

He didn't know what to do with the kinds of feelings that twisted inside him when he knew that nothing should have ever happened to her. She had been a normal girl, picking her father up from work, and she'd been kidnapped, measured and emotionally tortured into this bizarre world of being hidden away. Not touched, but put to work digging graves and hiding drugs.

"Don't you think?" she repeated, stepping closer to him.

She reached out to touch him and he sidestepped. He was too afraid if she touched him again, all of the certainty inside him would simply disappear and he would do something he would come to deeply regret. Something that would go against everything he'd been taught and everything he believed.

He was there to protect her, and that meant any deeper connection—physical or otherwise—was not ethical. It was screwing with a victim, and he wouldn't allow himself to fall that low. He had to keep a dispassionate consideration for her own good, not develop a passionate one.

"It's possible that evidence would be sufficient," he finally managed to say, his voice sounding raw. "But even if The Stallion goes to another compound, Layne and Wallace will still be here. Me doing any kind of digging is going to be hard to explain."

"Not if you told them that The Stallion ordered you to do it. He stays away for three months. So you'd have time before they'd tell him, wouldn't you?"

"I don't know how they communicate with

him when The Stallion isn't here. I'm sure there'd be a way for them to keep tabs on me, and we both know that's exactly what Layne will be doing whether he's supposed to be or not."

"What about Wallace?" Gabby demanded.

Jaime scratched a hand through his hair. "I don't think Wallace is the brightest, but he's the most loyal. Layne is out to get me. Wallace will do whatever it takes to protect The Stallion. Either way, I don't think I have much hope of getting anything past them. At least, not anything tangible like digging."

Noticing her shoulders slump, he hurried on.

"But that doesn't mean it's not useful information. Maybe we can't use it right this second to shut this whole thing down, but every last shred of evidence we have when we finally get to that point is another nail in The Stallion's coffin. Men like him—powerful, wealthy men with connections… They're not easy to take down. We need it all. So it's still important."

"Right. Well. What else could I tell you that would help?" she asked hopefully.

A million things, probably, but he thought distance might do them both a bit of good. Too close, too alone, too much…bed taking up a portion of the room. "Don't you want to sleep?" Because he wanted to convince himself sleep was why he was thinking about beds.

She looked at him curiously. "I haven't had much to do in eight years except sleep. Day in and day out."

"Right, but…" He struggled to find a rebuttal and failed.

The curious look on her face didn't disappear and he couldn't exactly analyze why he suddenly felt bizarrely nervous. He'd been prepared for a lot of things as an undercover FBI agent, but not what to do with nerves over a woman.

A woman he'd known for all of two days. Who knew his secret now, and was thus her own dangerous weapon, but even in his most suspicious mode, he couldn't believe she'd turn him in. They were each other's best hope.

"Is it hard to switch back and forth?" she asked earnestly.

"Switch back and forth?" He'd been so lost in his own thoughts he was having a hard time following hers.

"Between the real you and this character you have to play?"

"Are you sure they're so different?" He'd tried to say it somewhat sarcastically, or maybe even challengingly, but the minute it came out of his mouth, he knew what he really wanted to hear was that she could tell the difference. That she absolutely knew he was two separate people. Because if she could see it, if this stranger could see it, then maybe it was true. Maybe he really hadn't turned into someone else altogether.

"I've been nothing but Rodriguez for two years. You're the only one who knows any different. I don't know if it's easy. I only know that... This is the first time I've had to do it."

She stepped toward him again and he should sidestep again. He knew he should. Everything about Gabby called to him on a deep cellular level, though, and he didn't know how to keep fighting that call. There was only so much fighting a man could do.

She brushed her fingertips across his chest again. "Do you always wear these?"

Jaime looked down at the weapons strapped to his chest. "I try to. Not a lot of trustworthy men around."

Her fingertips traced the leather strap, which was strangely intimate considering the fact he never let anyone touch his weapons. It was a part of the persona he'd created. Slightly paranoid, always armed and always dangerous. No one touched his weapons.

Yet, he was letting her do just that. Touching them in ways she couldn't begin to understand he was touched.

"You could take them off in here." She looked up at him through the long spikes of her eyelashes.

It was tempting enough to lose his breath for a moment. "Wouldn't be smart," he rasped, surprised how visceral the reaction was to the thought of not being strapped to the hilt with guns and ammo. What would that feel like? He'd forgotten.

"Right. Of course not." She offered him a smile, something he supposed was an attempt at comfort, and that, too, was out of the ordinary. Something he didn't remember.

"I have to go."

"Why?"

He should lie. Tell her he had important henchman duties to see to, but the truth came out instead. "I can't stay in my own skin too long. It's too hard to go back otherwise."

Then she did the most incomprehensible thing of all. She rolled up on her tiptoes and brushed her lips across his cheek. His cheek. Soft and sweet. A soothing gesture. She came back down to be flat-footed and gave him a perilous smile.

"Then you should go. Good night, Jaime."

That, he knew, to be a challenge. He should correct her. Tell her that she absolutely had to call him Rodriguez. Lecture her until she wished he'd never come into her room.

Instead he returned her smile and said, "Good night, Gabby," before he left.

Chapter Eight

Gabby didn't know the last time she'd felt quite so light. Probably never here. It was probably warped.

Maybe if Jaime had showed up in her first year, it wouldn't be quite so easy to fall into comfort or friendship or even pseudo-flirting. Maybe there would have been enough of the real world and non-ghost Gabby to keep her distance or to keep her head straight.

But she had been here eight years, and all of those things before ceased to exist. All she had was these past eight years, and they had been dark and dreary and horrible. It was nice to have something to feel *light* about.

It didn't mean she wasn't worried about Natalie. It didn't mean she was happy to be kidnapped. It didn't mean a lot of things, but it did give her the opportunity to feel somewhat relaxed. To breathe. To smile as she thought of Jaime's bristled cheek under her mouth.

She made breakfast for the girls, which she did every Sunday. Even after she'd stopped counting the days, she made sure to know what days were Sundays so she could do this for them. Give them something, if not to look forward to, something that felt like this was home and not just prison.

She didn't know if any of them still believed in home. She didn't. This was a prison no matter what, but sometimes it was nice to feel like it wasn't.

"We've been talking," Alyssa announced

with no preamble, which was her usual way of broaching a subject. She had only been here for two years and one of the illuminating things about being imprisoned with other people was the realization that victims could be good and bad people themselves.

Alyssa was a bit of a jerk. Had been from the first moment, continued to be these two years later. She was too blunt and always abrasive, never kind to the softer girls. In real life, Gabby thought she might have ended up punching the woman in the nose.

But this wasn't real life.

"What about?" Gabby asked pleasantly, as if she cared.

"Rodriguez and his interest in you."

That certainly caught her off guard, but she feigned interest in her breakfast. "Interest?"

"He's traipsing in and out of your room at all hours."

Gabby slowly turned to face the trio of women in the exact same situation as her. They should be friends and yet all she felt like was an irritable babysitter. "Are you watching me, Alyssa?" Gabby asked, not bothering to soften the threat in her voice.

She wouldn't let anyone figure out what was going on, mostly because she didn't think the girls could hack it, but also because she didn't trust any of them. Perhaps same circumstances should have made them something like sisters, but when you were struck by senseless tragedy it was damn hard to remember to be empathetic toward anyone else.

"I've been watching *him*," Alyssa said with a sniff. "Are you sleeping with him?"

Gabby blinked. She couldn't tell if it was jealousy or fear or *what* that sparked Alyssa's interest. She only knew she was tired. Tired of navigating a world that didn't make any sense, and yet she barely remembered one that did.

She sighed. "The Stallion has *gifted* me to Rodriguez. I'm supposed to do whatever he wants." She almost smiled thinking about how surprised The Stallion would be to discover what Jaime really wanted.

Alyssa's eyes narrowed at the information but Jasmine gasped in horror and Tabitha looked frightened.

"Why you?" Alyssa demanded.

"I'm sorry, did you want to be offered up as payment for a job well done to any bad guy who walks through?" Gabby snapped.

Alyssa fidgeted, her expression losing a degree of its hostility. "Will it get you out?"

Gabby didn't know what to say. What little pieces of her heart that were left cracked hard for Alyssa thinking there was any possible way of getting out. And then there was the very fact that if anyone was ever going to get them out, it would be Jaime.

But not like Alyssa meant. "No," Gabby replied flatly. "Nothing we do for them gets us anything. We're things to them, at best. Certainly not people."

"What do we do then?" Jasmine asked, her voice wobbly and close to tears.

"We wait for him to die," Tabitha said morosely, lowering herself to a seat.

Jasmine sniffled and sat next to Tabitha, but Alyssa still stood, staring at the girls and then at Gabby. "Maybe we hurry that along."

Gabby's eyebrows winged up. It wasn't that she'd never wondered what it might take to kill The Stallion and escape on her own. It was just… She never thought the other women would have the same thoughts.

But Alyssa's face was grim and impassive, and the other girls were contemplatively silent.

"There's four of them, though," Tabitha offered in a whisper, as though they were plotting and not merely…thinking aloud.

"And four of us," Gabby murmured. A few days ago she would have shut this conversation down. She would have reminded them all that there was no hope and they might as well make the best of their fates.

She would have been wrong. Wrong to squash their hope, and their fight, like she'd been wrong to squash her own.

Jaime had brought it back, had reminded her that life did in fact exist outside these walls. Natalie, on the run. Blue skies. Freedom.

A dangerous kind of hope built in her chest. An aching, desperate need for that freedom she'd tried to forget existed. Even as Jaime had talked of ends and bringing him down, she had tried to fight this feeling away.

But it was all his fault she'd lost the reserves, because he'd appeared out of nowhere and trusted her in his mission. He'd somehow crashed into her world and opened her up *to* life again, not just existence.

"How would we do it?" Tabitha asked, her eyes darting around the kitchen nervously.

Alyssa eyed Gabby still. "Rodriguez wears a lot of guns, and if you are a gift, it means he gets awfully close to you."

"I couldn't steal his gun without him noticing."

Alyssa shrugged easily. "That doesn't mean you couldn't get it and shoot before he had a chance to notice."

The three women looked at her expectantly and she wondered if they hadn't all gone a little crazy. "Or, he stops me and shoots me first."

Alyssa raised a delicate shoulder. "Maybe it'd be worth the risk."

"Then you risk it," Jasmine said, surprising

Gabby by doing a little standing up for her. "It was your idea, after all."

This time Alyssa smirked. "But Gabby is the one with access to his *guns*."

Gabby couldn't think of what to say to that. She had access to a lot of things, but she couldn't and didn't trust Alyssa with the information, and she wasn't sure she could trust Jasmine or Tabitha, either. All it would take was one woman to slip up or break and Jaime could end up dead.

It wasn't safe to let them into this, and it wasn't fair to refuse these women some hope, some power.

Leave it to Alyssa to make an already complicated, somewhat dangerous, situation even more twisted.

Gabby took a deep breath and tried to smile in some appropriate way. Scheming or interested or whatever, not irritated and nervous. Not…guilty. "I'll see what I can do, okay?"

"Don't put yourself in harm's way, Gabby," Jasmine said softly. "What would we do without you?"

Alyssa snorted derisively, but Gabby pretended she didn't notice and smiled reassuringly at Jasmine. "I'll be careful," she promised.

A whole lot of careful.

JAIME STOOD IN the corner of The Stallion's well-lit shed while the man paced and raged at the news Wallace had just delivered.

"How did they get away? How did my men get arrested? I demand answers." He pounded on his desk, the dolls shaking perilously, like little train wrecks Jaime couldn't stop staring at.

"I don't know," Wallace said, shrinking back.

"I guess the Ranger tangled 'em up with the local cops."

The Stallion whirled on Wallace. "Who is this Ranger?"

"Er, his name's V-Vaughn Cooper. With the unsolved c-crimes unit. Uh—"

Jaime lost track of whatever The Stallion's sharp demand was at the name. Vaughn Cooper. He *knew* Vaughn Cooper. Ranger Cooper had taught a class Jaime had taken in the police academy.

Christ.

"Rodriguez." It took Jaime a few full seconds to engage, to remember who and where he was. Not a kid in the police academy. Not an FBI agent. Rodriguez.

"¿Senor?" he offered, damning himself for his voice coming out rusty.

"No. Not you. Not yet." The Stallion muttered, wild eyes bouncing from Jaime to the other men. "Wallace. Layne. You find them. You track them down. The girl, you bring to me. The Ranger, I don't give a damn about. Do what you will."

Layne grinned a little maniacally at that and Jaime knew he had to do something. He couldn't let Cooper get caught in some sort of ambush. He couldn't let a man who'd reminded them all to, above all else, maintain their humanity, get killed. Especially with Gabby's sister.

"*Senor*, perhaps you could allow me to take care of this problem." He smiled blandly at Layne. "I might be better suited to such a task."

The Stallion gave him a considering once-over. "Perhaps." He paced, looking up at his collection of dolls then running a long finger down the line of one's foot.

Jaime barely fought the grimace.

"No, I want you here, Rodriguez. We have things to discuss."

That wasn't exactly a comfort, though he did remind himself that as long as he was here, Gabby was safe. He wasn't so sure Layne would leave her be if Jaime wasn't around, even with The Stallion's distaste over hurting women.

Jaime assured himself Ranger Cooper knew what he was doing, prayed he knew what he was up against. If the man had outwitted the first two of The Stallion's men, surely he could outwit Wallace and Layne.

"You have three days to bring her to me. The consequences if you fail will be dire. I would get started immediately."

The other two men rushed to do their boss's bidding, hurrying out of the shed, heads bent together as they strategized.

Jaime remained still, trying to hide any nerves, any concern, with cool disinterest.

The Stallion turned to him, studying him in the eerie silence for far too long.

"I hope you're being careful with our Gabriella," The Stallion said at last.

"Careful?" Jaime forced himself to smile slyly. He spread his arms wide, palms up to the ceiling. "Care was not part of our bargain, *senor.*"

The Stallion waved that away. "No, I'm not talking about being gentle. I'm talking about being *careful.* Condoms and whatnot."

Jaime stared blankly at the man. Was he... giving him sort of a sex-ed talk?

"Women carry diseases, you know." The Stallion continued as though this was a normal topic of conversation. "And she's not a virgin, according to her."

"I..." Jaime couldn't get the rest of the words

out of his strangled throat. The "according to her" should be some kind of comfort, but why had the man been quizzing her on the state of her virginity? Why did he think Jaime—er, Rodriguez, would care?

"Perfect in every way, save for that," The Stallion said, shaking his head sadly. "Oh, well, then there were her toes."

"Her...toes?"

"The middle one is longer than the big toe. Unnatural." The Stallion shuddered before running his fingers over his dolls' feet again.

Jaime knew he didn't hide his bewilderment very well, but it was nearly impossible to school away. What on earth went through this man's head? He ran corporations. Jaime doubted very much anyone in Austin knew Victor Callihan was really a madman. Perhaps eccentric, somewhat scarce when it came to social situations, but he was still *known*. Somehow he could hide all this…whatever it was, warped in his head.

"Regardless, if you are to be my right-hand man, and insist upon indulging in these baser instincts inferior men have, I expect you to keep yourself clean."

"I… *Sí*." What the hell else was there to say?

"Good. Now, I held you back because I have some concerns I didn't want to broach in front of Layne and Wallace. I think we've been infiltrated."

There was a cold burst of fear deep within Jaime's gut, but on the outside he merely lifted an eyebrow. "Where?"

"Here," The Stallion said grimly, tapping his desk. "I don't believe that Ranger was smart enough to outwit my men unless he was tipped off. This is why I sent Layne and kept you with me."

"I do not follow."

The Stallion sighed exhaustedly. "You're lucky you're such a good shot, but I suppose I wouldn't want anyone too smart under me. How could I trust them to follow my lead?" He shook his head. "Anyway, if Layne and Wallace fail, I will be assured it's one of them, and they'll be taken care of. If they succeed, then I know my suspicions are wrong and we can carry on."

Jaime inclined his head and breathed a very quiet sigh of relief.

"If they fail, you will be in charge of punishing them suitably." The Stallion frowned down at his desk. "I don't like to alter my schedule…"

"If there's somewhere you need to be, I can be in charge here. I can mete out whatever punishments necessary, gladly."

The Stallion made a noise in the back of his throat. "This situation is priority number one. I need to do some investigating into this Ranger, and I want to be here for the arrival of Gabriella's sister to do my initial testing. For now, you're free to fill your time with our Gabriella. Get it out of your system before her sister gets here, if you would, please."

Jaime bowed faintly as if in agreement.

"You did give her my message, didn't you?" The Stallion asked, his gaze sharp and assessing.

"Sí."

"And how did she react? Were there tears?"

The Stallion sounded downright ecstatic, so Jaime lied. *"Sí."*

He sighed happily. "I should have done it myself, though I do like you telling her and then doing whatever it is you must do with her. Yes, that's a nice punishment for the little slut."

Jaime bit down on his tongue, hard, a sharp

reminder that defending anyone wasn't necessary, no matter how much it felt it was.

"May I go, *senor*?" he asked through clenched teeth.

The Stallion inclined his head. "Do what you can to make her cry again. Yes, I like the idea of proud Gabriella crying every night. And when her sister comes…well, I'll bear witness to that."

All Jaime could think as he left the shed was *like hell he would.*

Chapter Nine

Gabby didn't see Jaime all day. She'd expected him—to pop into her room, to come into the kitchen at dinner, something. But she'd eaten with the girls nearly an hour ago and she'd been in her room ever since…waiting.

She shouldn't be edgy, yet she couldn't help herself. The more time she had alone—or worse, with the other girls—the more her mind turned over the possibility of actually killing a man.

Actually escaping.

But she had Jaime for that, didn't she? Alyssa's cold certainty haunted Gabby, though. Should she have thought of this before? Not just as angry outbursts, but as a true, honest-to-God possibility?

Of course, this was the first time in eight years Gabby'd had access to anything that might act as a viable weapon. If she could count Jaime and his guns as accessible.

Where was he? And what was he doing? Had The Stallion sent him on some errand? Was he gone for good?

Her heart stuttered at that thought. Somehow it had never occurred to her that something might happen to him or that he might get sent elsewhere, but Layne and Wallace, and the other three men who sometimes guarded them were forever leaving for intervals of time. Some never to return.

Oh, God, what if he never came back and she'd missed all her chances? What if she was stuck here forever? What if all that hope had been a worthless waste of—

Her door inched open and Jaime stepped inside, sunglasses covering his eyes, weapons strapped to his chest. Strong and capable and *there*.

She very nearly ran to him, to touch him and assure herself he was real and not a figment of her imagination.

The only thing that stopped her was the fact that in three short days she'd come to rely on this man, expect this man, and in just a few minutes she'd reminded herself why she couldn't let that happen.

He could be shipped out. He could be executed. Anything—*anything* could happen to him and if she didn't make a move to protect herself and Jasmine, Alyssa and Tabitha... they'd all be out in the cold.

She tamped down the fear that made her nauseous. Jaime seemed to remind her of the best and worst things. Hope. Freedom. An end to this hell. Then how it could all be taken away.

"I have a bit of good news for you," he said, slipping his glasses off and into his pocket.

Some of the fear coiled inside her released of its own accord. It was so hard to fear when she could see his dark brown eyes search her face as if she held some answer for him. Some comfort.

"Okay," she said carefully, because she wasn't sure she had any for him.

"Your sister and the Texas Ranger she's with escaped The Stallion's first round of men."

"First...round."

"And I know the Texas Ranger she's with. He's a good man. A good police officer."

"But he's sending another round of men," Gabby said dully, because though she'd not spent a lot of time with The Stallion, she knew his habits. She knew what he did and what he saw. When he saw a challenge, he didn't back down.

"Layne and Wallace," Jaime confirmed, crossing to where she sat on her bed. He crouched in front of her and, after a moment, took her hands in his. "I tried to get him to send me, but he thinks Layne is leaking things to the cops."

Gabby jerked her gaze up from where it had been on their joined hands. "He thinks there's a leak," she gasped. That meant Jaime was in danger. That meant once The Stallion figured out it wasn't Layne, he'd figure out it was Jaime and then—

Jaime squeezed her hands. "I don't actually think he thinks that because of anything I've done. He thinks it too convenient that Ranger Cooper and your sister outwitted those men, but he's underestimating the Ranger."

"Maybe he's underestimating my sister."

Jaime smiled, and not even one of those comforting ones. No, this seemed closer to genuine. A real feeling, not one born of this place. It smoothed through her like a warm drink on a cold day, which she barely remembered as a thing, but his smile made her remember.

"Maybe that is it. He certainly underestimates you."

"But you don't." She touched his cheek, brushed her fingertips across his bristled jaw. Five seconds in his company and she'd forgotten all the admonitions she'd just made to herself. But in his presence—calm and strong and comforting—she forgot everything.

Her gaze dropped to the weapons strapped to his chest and she sighed. Well, not everything. Alyssa's words were still there, scrambling around in her brain.

She dropped her fingers from his face to his

holster of weapons. She traced her hand over a gun. She didn't know anything about guns. He'd have to somehow teach her to fire one, and it wasn't as if she'd be able to practice anywhere.

But maybe one of the other girls knew how to shoot. If she got one to them…?

She sighed, overwhelmed. This was why she'd given up making a plan. Too many variables. She could analyze a problem, remember a million facts and figures, puzzle together disparate pieces, but when it came to all the unknown fallout of her possible actions…

It made her want to curl up in her bed and cry.

"What's wrong?"

She had to put it all away. Emotion had never gotten her anything in this place. Unless it was anger. Unless it was fight.

"Would they notice?" she forced herself to

say strongly and evenly. "If you gave one of these to me, would anyone notice it missing?"

His expression changed into something she didn't recognize. Into something almost like suspicion. "You want one of my guns?" he asked, moving out of his crouch and into a standing position. He folded his arms across his chest and looked down at her, and it was a wonder anyone who really paid attention didn't see the way his demeanor screamed *law enforcement*.

"What do you want to do with it?" he asked carefully, the same way she thought he might interrogate a criminal.

She wasn't sure what she'd expected, but she didn't like *that*. Trust was a two-way street, wasn't it? Didn't he have to trust her for her to trust him?

"What's going on, Gabby?"

She looked away from his dark brown gaze,

from the arms-crossed, FBI-agent posture. She looked away from the man she didn't know. Hard and very nearly uncompromising.

She shouldn't tell him about the girls' plan. It felt like a violation of privacy, and yet, if she kept it from him he could just as easily be hurt, or accidentally hurt one of the girls.

It was a no-win situation, which should feel familiar. She'd been living "no win" for eight years.

Then his finger traced her cheek, so feather-light, before he paused under her chin, tilting her head up so she would look at him.

She was tired of hard things and no-win situations and *this*. But Jaime… It was as though he looked at her as neither just another kidnapping victim nor as the strong leader, not as anything but herself.

"What do you know about me, Jaime?" she asked, not even sure where the question came from but knowing she needed an answer. She needed something.

He cocked his head, but he didn't ask her to explain herself. Instead he pulled her up into a standing position, gripping her shoulders and staring down into her eyes. Everything about him intense and strong and just...*him*.

"I know you're brilliant. That you're beyond strong. I know you love your family, and it eats at you that you can't protect Natalie from this. I know you've been hurt, and you're tired. But I also know you'll endure, because there is something inside of you that cannot be killed. No matter what that man does. You're a fighter."

It was a torrent of words. Positive attributes she'd thought about herself, questioned about herself. All said in that brook-no-argument, no-nonsense tone, his gaze never leaving hers. She knew he had to be a good liar to have survived undercover for two years, and yet she couldn't believe this was anything but the truth.

Jaime saw who she was—not what she'd done or how long she'd been here. He saw her. In all the different ways she was.

"The girls want to—" Gabby swallowed. She had to trust him. She did, because he was her only hope, and because he saw her like no one else had in eight years. "They want me to try to get a gun from you, and then go after The Stallion."

Jaime's forehead scrunched. "They can't do that."

"Why not?" she demanded, something like panic pumping through her. She wanted to be out of there. She wanted a *life*. Even if it wasn't her old life, she wanted…

Him. She wanted him in the real world, and she wanted her.

"I'm here to take him down, Gabby. I'm here

to make sure he goes to jail, not just for justice, but so we can put an end to all the evil this man is doing. We can't shoot him in a blaze of glory. That just leaves a power vacuum someone else can take."

"I don't care," she whispered, feeling too close to tears for even her own comfort. But she didn't care in the least. The Stallion was going after her sister and she just wanted him *dead*.

"I understand that. I do. But—"

"My freedom isn't your fight." She sat back down on the bed, slipping through his strong grasp. He could see her. Maybe he even felt some of the things she felt, but her fight was not his fight.

He crouched again, not letting her pull into herself. He took her hands and he waited, silent and patient, until she raised her wary gaze to his.

"It's part of my fight," he said, not just earnestly but vehemently, fervently. "It's a part I don't intend to fail on. I will get you out of here. I will. But I need to do my job, too. It is why I'm here."

A tear slipped out, and then another, and she felt so stupid for crying in front of him, but everything ached in a way she hadn't let it for a very long time.

He brushed one tear off with his thumb then he leaned forward, his mouth so close she inhaled sharply, drowning a little in his dark eyes, wanting to get lost in the warm strength of his body.

"Don't cry," he said on a whisper before he brushed his mouth against another tear, wiping it from her jaw with his mouth.

He pulled his face away from hers, shaking his head. "I shouldn't—"

But she didn't want his shouldn'ts and she

didn't want him to pull away, so she tugged him closer and covered his mouth with hers.

HE'D DREAMED OF THIS. Gabby's mouth under his again. Not because he was trying to be someone else. Not because he was trying to convince *anyone* he was taking what he wanted.

No, he'd dreamed of her mouth touching his because they'd both wanted it, not from anything born of this place. On the outside. Free. Themselves. He'd imagined it, unable to help himself.

Even having dreamed of it, even in the midst of allowing it to happen in the here and now, he knew it was wrong. Not just against everything he'd ever been taught in his law-enforcement training, but against things he believed.

She was a victim. No matter how strong she was. No matter how much he felt for her. She was still a victim of this place. Kissing her, drowning in it, was like taking advantage of her. It was wrong. It flew in the face of who he was as an FBI agent, as a law-enforcement agent.

But he didn't stop. Couldn't. Because while it went against all those things he was, it didn't go against who he was. Deep down, this was all he wanted.

Her tongue traced his mouth and she sighed against him. Melting, leaning. Crawling under all the defenses he wound around himself. False identities. Badges and pledges. Weapons and uniforms and lies.

He should pull away. He should stop this madness.

He curled his fingers into her soft hair. He angled her head so that he could taste her better. He ignored every last voice in his head telling him to stop. Because she was touching him. Tracing the line of his shoulders. Pressing her hand to his heart. She scooted closer, brushing her chest against his.

She whispered his name against his mouth. His real name. And he wanted to be able to be that. He wanted to be able to be the man who could give her everything she wanted and everything she deserved.

But he wasn't that man. Not here. Not now. He couldn't even let her have fantasies of ending The Stallion's life.

He mustered all of his strength and all of his righteous rightness. Somehow…*somehow* he did the thing he least wanted to do and pulled away from her.

Her breath was coming in heavy pants, as was his. Her dark eyes were unfathomably warm, her lips wet from his mouth. He wanted to sink himself there again and again until they thought of nothing but each other.

"Jaime," she said on a whisper.

"We can't do this. I can't…" He tried to pull away but her arms were strong around him.

"Do you know how long it's been since someone's kissed me? Since I *wanted* someone to kiss me?"

"Gabby," he returned, pained. Desperate—for her and a way this could be right.

"I know it isn't the time or the place. I know it isn't prudent or whatever, but I have lived here for eight years without anything I wanted. I survived here without anyone touching me kindly, comfortingly or wanting to. Without anyone seeing me as anything other than a *thing*. If I'm going to believe in an *end*, I have to believe I can go back to being something real, not just this…ghost of a person."

"Getting involved with the victim is not an acceptable—"

She pulled away from him quickly and with

absolutely no hesitation. She turned her head away, shaking it. He'd stepped in it, badly.

"I know you don't want to see yourself as a victim," he began, trying to resist the impulse to reach for her. "But in my line of work—"

"I understand."

But she didn't understand. She was angry and she didn't understand at all. "I do know how you feel," he offered softly.

She rolled her eyes.

"It hasn't been eight years, but two years is a long time to go without anyone seeing you for who you are. There aren't a lot of hugs and nice words for the bad guy, Gabby. Even the *other* bad guys don't like me because I've been slowly taking them down so that I could be the one next to The Stallion. It isn't all fun and games over here."

"Are you asking me to feel sorry for you?" she asked incredulously.

"Of course not." He raked a hand through his hair, trying to figure out what he *was* trying to ask of her. "I'm saying that I understand. I'm saying that I would love to give you what you want. I would…"

"I'm just a victim. And you can't get involved with the victim. I get it."

"You don't, because if you thought it was that simple… I have never in my entire career even considered kissing someone who was involved with a case I was part of. I have never once been unable to stop thinking about a woman who had anything to do with *work*. I have never been remotely—*remotely*—tempted to go against everything I believe. Until you."

That seemed to dilute at least some of her anger. She still didn't look at him, which was maybe for the best. He wasn't sure if she looked at him that he'd be able to stay noble.

Because her soft lips tempted him. And the

defiant look in her eyes… Everything about her was very near impossible to resist.

He hadn't been lying that he'd never wanted someone the way he wanted her. Even if he took the police part out of it. No woman, no matter how short or long a period of time they had been in his life, had made him feel the way Gabby made him feel.

He wondered if that wasn't why she was upset. Not that he'd stopped the kiss, but that she thought he didn't see her the way he did.

She'd asked what he knew about her, and he'd been completely honest and open about all the things he *knew* she was. Maybe he shouldn't have been, but she was everything he'd said, and he knew being attracted to her, caring about her, wasn't as simple as whatever label a therapist would likely put on it.

It was Gabby, not the situation, that called to

him. But the situation was what made every-thing far too complicated.

"I can't give you a weapon," he offered into her stubborn silence.

"All right," she said, and she didn't sound angry. She sounded tired. Very close to giving up. But then she straightened her shoulders and inhaled and exhaled slowly. Then she met his gaze, fierce and strong.

"I have to have a story for the girls...I have to... They want out, Jaime." Something in her face changed, a kind of empathetic pain. "I used to be able to tell them it wasn't any use to think about getting out, but we can't keep doing this. Alyssa is right. Staying here isn't worth being alive for."

"So what kept you alive for so long?" he asked because he couldn't imagine. He couldn't *fathom*.

"My family, I guess. Daddy died because

of his guilt over me. The least I could do was still be alive. The least I could do was get back somehow." She looked down at her hands, clenched in her lap. "I thought I'd given up that hope, but I don't know. Maybe I just convinced myself I had."

He covered her clenched fists with his own. "I'm going to get you back to your family." God, he'd do it. Come hell or high water. If he had to *die* first, he would do it.

"Not so long ago you said you couldn't promise me that."

"Not so long ago I was doing everything by the book." He believed in the book, but he also…he also believed in this woman. "You're right. Things can't stand. It's been too long. We can't keep waiting around. We have to make something happen."

She finally looked at him, eyebrows raised. "Really?"

"As soon as we get word that your sister has escaped Layne and Wallace, we'll…" It was against everything he'd been taught, everything he was supposed to do, but he couldn't keep telling Gabby to wait when he could be getting her out.

"Once we know your sister is safe, we'll figure out an escape plan. You can't tell the others who I am but… Maybe you can tell them I'm sympathetic, if you trust them to keep that to themselves. Tell them that if you work on me for a few days, you might actually be able to get a weapon from me. If anything slips up to The Stallion or anyone else, I'll tell him it's part of my plan. If you get the girls to stand down a few days. I don't want to risk getting out and something happening to your sister."

"Why?" she asked, still studying him, her forehead creased.

"Because you love her."

Something in her face changed and he couldn't read it. But she moved. Closer to him. No matter that he should absolutely avoid it, he let her kiss him again.

Slow and leisurely, as if they had all the time in the world. As if it was just the two of them. Gabby and Jaime. As if that were possible.

And because the thought was so tempting, so comforting in this world of dark, horrible things, he let it linger far too long.

Chapter Ten

Gabby had kissed four men in her life. Ricky, of course. Corey Gentry on a dare in eighth grade. A guy at a frat party—she didn't know his name—and now Jaime.

In the past eight years she would've considered this part of her dead. The part that could care about kissing and touching. The part of her brain that could go from that to sex.

It was a miracle and a joy to still have the same kind of desire she'd had before. It was a miracle and a joy to be kissing Jaime, his lips so soft, his touch nearly reverent. As though she were something of a miracle to him.

Ricky had never kissed her like this and she'd been convinced she loved him. But he'd been a boy and she'd been a girl. They'd been selfish and Jaime… Jaime was anything but selfish. A good man. A strong and honorable man.

That somehow made the kiss more exciting, knowing he thought it was wrong but couldn't quite help himself. Knowing he felt the same simmering feelings and that he didn't think it was because of their situation. It was because of who they were.

Gabby. Jaime.

She thought she hadn't known who she was anymore, but she was learning. Jaime was showing her pieces of herself she'd forgotten. He was bending his strict moral code for her and that, above all else, spoke to a feeling most people wouldn't believe could happen in three days. She herself wasn't sure she'd believed something like this could grow in three days.

But here she was feeling things for a man that she'd never felt before. She wanted to be able to make sacrifices for him, and she wanted him safe, and she wanted him *hers*.

He pulled away slightly and it was another wondrous thing that every time he pulled away she could *feel* how hard it was for him to do so.

"I have a meeting with The Stallion," he said, his voice very nearly hoarse. "I can't be late again or things could get ugly." He tried to smile, probably to make it sound less intimidating, but it didn't work.

She clutched him harder. "Come back," she blurted. She said it spontaneously, but she still meant it. She wanted him to come back. She wanted more than a kiss.

"So we can…" He cleared his throat. "Plan, right?"

She smiled at him because it was cute he would even think that. "We can plan, too." She watched him swallow as though he were nervous. She didn't mind that the least little bit.

"Gabby."

"Come back tonight. Spend the night with me."

It was a wonderful thing to know he wanted to. That though he was resisting, something deep inside him wanted to or he wouldn't question it at all. It was so against his inner sense of right and wrong, but he wouldn't fight with that if he didn't truly want her.

"It wouldn't be right. To… It would be taking advantage," he said, as though trying to convince himself.

"You're worried about me taking advantage of you?" she asked as innocently as she could manage.

He laughed, low and rumbly. It struck her that this was the first time she'd heard it, possibly one of the very few times she'd heard nice laughter in *years*.

"Gabby, you've been through hell for eight years."

As if she needed the reminder. "I guess that's all the more reason to know exactly what I want," she said resolutely. She knew what she wanted and if she could have it… If she could have him… She'd do it now. She wouldn't waste time. "I want you, Jaime."

He inhaled sharply, but he didn't say anything. "I have to go," he said, getting to his feet.

She gave him a nod, but she thought he'd be back. She really thought he'd return to her. Because he felt it, too. He had to feel it, too. No matter how warped she sometimes felt, this was the most real she'd felt in eight years. The most honest and the most true. The most certain she could survive getting out of this hell. That she wanted to.

That settled inside her like some weird evangelical itch. She wanted to be able to give that same feeling to the other girls. They deserved something, too. Something to believe in. They hadn't spent as much time as her, no, but they had spent enough. They had all spent enough.

Jaime was willing to break the rules and get them there, as soon as Natalie was safe. Not because that helped him any, but because she loved her sister and he knew that meant something to her.

Gabby left her room. She didn't know where exactly Jaime had gone, but she wasn't after him quite now. First, she wanted to find Alyssa. She wanted everyone to know that she was on board, maybe not in the way they thought, but regardless. They were going to find a way out of this.

She walked into the common room, which was basically their workroom opposite the kitchen and dining area.

Tabitha and Jasmine were sitting on the dilapidated couch working on a project The Stallion had assigned them a few days ago. Gabby realized she'd forgotten all about the project and what her role in it was supposed to have been. But ever since Jaime had arrived, it hadn't even occurred to her. Then again, she supposed to The Stallion her job now was to be payment to Jaime. Though she was surprised the girls hadn't asked her for help.

Jasmine looked at her first, eyes wide. She looked from Alyssa, who was riffling through drawers frantically in the kitchen, back to Gabby.

"Did you…?" she whispered then trailed off.

Gabby nodded. "I didn't get a gun or anything, but I think I can. If you give me some time." There was hope. She needed to give them hope.

Alyssa slammed a cabinet door closed and stormed over to them. "What does that mean?" she demanded.

"It means I couldn't quite sneak a weapon off of him, but he seemed a little…sympathetic almost. Like if I keep feeding him our sob story he might…"

"What you really need to do is willingly sleep with him, not fight him off," Alyssa said flatly, giving her a once-over. "When he thinks you're not fighting him, it'll give you time to grab his gun and shoot him."

Gabby couldn't hide a shudder. Maybe if they'd been talking about any of the other men, she wouldn't have felt an icy horror over Alyssa's words. But this was Jaime. Still, she couldn't let even the other girls think he'd gotten to her.

She forced herself to look at Alyssa evenly. "And then what?"

"What do you mean and then what?" Alyssa demanded.

"There are at least three other men here almost at all times. What do you suggest I do after I shoot him? I'm pretty sure gunshots can be heard somewhere else in this little compound, then one of them is going to come running to shoot me. They've got a little more experience with guns and killing people than I do."

Alyssa pressed her lips together, neither mollified nor understanding.

"You just have to give me some time," Gabby said, trying for calm and in charge. "If not to convince him to give me a weapon, then at least time to find a way to sneak one off him without him noticing right away. We do this without a plan, without thinking everything through, then we're all dead. You can't just…"

Alyssa's face was even more mutinous, turning red almost. Gabby tried for conciliatory, though it grated at her a bit. "I know we all want out." She looked at Tabitha and Jasmine, who were watching everything play out from where they sewed on the couch. "And I know once you start thinking about all of the things you could do once you got out of here that it builds inside you and everything feels… Too much. You start to panic. But if we are going to survive getting out of here, we have to be smart. Okay?"

"Does it matter if we survive?" Alyssa asked, all but snarling at Gabby.

Jasmine gasped and Tabitha straightened.

"Of course it matters," Tabitha shouted from the couch. She took in a deep, tremulous breath, calming herself as Jasmine patted her arm. "I'd rather be alive and here for the next *ten* years than die and never get a chance to see my family again." Her voice wavered but she kept going. "We have to have patience, and we have to do this smart. This is the first time any of us has access to a weapon, and we can't waste the chance. It won't happen again. At least, not for a very long time."

Alyssa scoffed, but she didn't pose any more arguments. "I'm going crazy in this place," she muttered, hugging herself.

"Why don't you help us work?" Jasmine offered. "I know it isn't any fun, but it'll at least keep your mind busy."

"You two can be his slave. I have no interest."

Tabitha and Jasmine exchanged an eye-roll and Alyssa stomped back to the kitchen. She riffled through the drawers again, inspecting butter knives and forks.

Gabby hoped Natalie and her Ranger escaped The Stallion's men once and for all, and quickly. Not just for her own sake, and for Jaime's, but because she wasn't certain Alyssa would last much longer.

If she didn't last, if she kept being something of a loose cannon, then they were all in danger. Including Jaime.

Jaime didn't go to Gabby that night. He knew it was cowardly to avoid her. He also knew it was for the best. For both of them. He wouldn't be able to resist what she offered, and it wasn't fair to take it. So he kept himself away, falling into a fitful sleep that was never quite restful.

The next day he busied himself outside. He fed The Stallion a story about wanting to come up with some new security tactics, but what he was really trying to do was to see if he could find any evidence of a shallow grave.

The Stallion was so obsessed with Layne and Wallace's progress in finding Ranger Cooper and Gabby's sister, Jaime felt pretty confident he could get away with a lot of things today.

Including going to see Gabby for only personal reasons.

He shook the thought away as he toed some dirt in the front yard. Unfortunately the entire area, especially in the front, was nothing but hardscrabble existence. Scrub brush and tall, thick weeds. It was impossible to tell if things had been dug, if things had grown over, if empty patches of land were a sign of a grave or just bad soil.

Being irritated with himself over his inability to find a lead didn't stop him from continuing to do it.

Until he heard the scream. A howling, broken sound. Keening almost. Coming from inside. From a woman.

"Gabby," he said aloud.

He forgot what he'd been doing and ran full-speed to the front door. He struggled with the chains on the doors and cursed them. It took him precious minutes to realize the door wasn't just locked and chained, it had been sealed shut with something. There was no possible way of getting to her through this door. He swore even louder and rushed around to the back.

Was The Stallion inside or in his shed? Was he hurting them? Jaime grabbed one of the guns from his chest. If he was hurting Gabby—if he was hurting any of them—this was over. Jaime wasn't going to let that happen. Not for anything. Not for any damn evidence to be used in a useless trial.

He'd just kill him and be done with it.

Nearly sweating, Jaime finally got all the locks and chains undone. He hadn't heard another scream and didn't know if that was a good or bad sign. He ran down the hall, looking in every open door. Gabby wasn't in her room and it prompted him to run faster.

He reached the main room and skidded to a halt at the sight before him. Gabby was standing there in the center of the room looking furious, blood dripping down her nose.

"What the hell happened?" he demanded, searching the room and only seeing the other women.

Gabby's gaze snapped to his and she widened her eyes briefly, as if to remind him he had an identity to maintain. It wasn't Demanding FBI Agent. *Or concerned...whatever you are.*

Either way, he'd forgotten. He'd let fear make him reckless. He'd let worry slip his mask. He very well could have ruined everything if not for that little flick of a gaze from Gabby.

He took a breath, calming the erratic beating

of his heart. He moved his gaze from Gabby's bloody face, fighting every urge to grab her and pat her down himself to make sure she wasn't hurt anywhere else.

"Well, *senoritas*?" he demanded, rolling his R's in as exaggerated a manner as he could manage in his current state. He glared at the other three women. The two blondes were holding the brunette down on the couch.

The brunette was breathing heavily, her nostrils flaring as she glared at Gabby. Slowly, she took her gaze off Gabby and let it rest on him.

She sneered and then spat. Right on one of the girls holding her. The slighter blonde shrieked and jumped back, which gave the brunette time to throw off the other woman and jump to her feet.

It wasn't wasted on him that Gabby immediately went into a fighter stance.

"First shot was free, but you hit me again, I

will beat you," she said, angry and menacing as the brunette stepped toward her.

Jaime stepped between them. "I will say this only once more. What is going on?" He realized he was still holding his gun and gestured it at the angry brunette threateningly.

The girl who'd been spit on squeaked and cowered while the girl who'd been flung off the brunette turned an even paler shade of white.

"Let's have story time, Alyssa. Tell our captor here what you're after," Gabby goaded.

"I'm going to get out of here," Alyssa yelled, whirling from Jaime to the blondes. "I don't care if I kill all of you." She pointed around him at Gabby. "I am going to get the hell out of here."

Jaime didn't want to feel sorry for the girl considering she was clearly at fault for Gabby's bloody nose, but he looked at Gabby and watched her shoulders slump and the fury in her eyes dim.

Damn it. He couldn't blame the woman for losing her mind here. Not in the least. But it was the last thing they needed if they were actually going to put something in motion that might get them out.

"You would be dead before you killed anyone, *senorita*. Calm yourself."

She bared her teeth at him. "I can't do this anymore. I can't do this anymore. Shoot me." She lunged toward him. "God, put me out of my misery."

"Hush," he ordered flatly, tamping down every possible empathetic feeling rising up inside him. "I'm not going to kill you. And you are not going to kill anyone. You're going to calm yourself."

"Or what? What happens if I don't?" She got

close enough to shove him, even reached out to do it, but Gabby was stepping between them.

Jaime was certain the woman would throw another punch at Gabby and he would have to intervene, but Gabby did the most incomprehensible thing. She pulled the woman into a hug.

And the woman began to sob.

The others started, too. All four of them crying, Gabby with her nose still bleeding.

Jaime had to clench his free hand into a fist and pray for some kind of composure. It was too much, these poor women, taken from their lives and expected to somehow endure it.

"What is all this?" The Stallion demanded and Jaime was such a fool he actually jumped. Where had all his instincts gone? All his self-preservation? He'd lost it, all because Gabby had gotten under his skin.

Jaime steeled himself and turned to face The Stallion.

"Your charges were getting out of hand. I had to do some knocking around," Jaime offered, nodding at Gabby's nose. If any of the girls wanted to refute his story, it would possibly end his life.

But none of them did.

"She is mine, no?" Jaime continued, hoping the fact Gabby was a gift meant he'd forgive him for the supposed violence that had shed blood.

The Stallion was staring oddly at Gabby, and it took everything in Jaime's power not to step between them. In an obvious way. Instead he simply angled his body and hoped like hell it wasn't obvious how much he wanted to protect her.

"Crying," The Stallion said in a kind of wondering tone. "Well, I am impressed, Rodriguez. No one has ever gotten her to cry."

Gabby flipped him the finger and Jaime nearly broke. Nearly ended it all right there.

"I trust our friend has told you that your sister will be joining us soon," The Stallion said, watching her far too carefully no matter how Jaime tried to angle himself into the picture.

"And yet she isn't here yet. Why is that?" Gabby returned in an equally conversational tone.

Jaime might have fallen in love with her right there.

The Stallion, however, snarled. "You're lucky I don't want to touch your disease-ridden body. But I have found someone who will. Take her away from me, Rodriguez. I don't want to see that face until her sister is here. Make sure to lock her room once you're done with her. She's done with outside privileges."

"And these?" Jaime managed to ask.

The Stallion snapped his fingers. "To your rooms. Don't make me turn you into gifts, as well."

The girls, even the instigator, scattered quickly.

The Stallion squinted at Gabby and maybe it was her unwillingness to cower or to jump that made her a target.

If Gabby cared about that, she didn't show it. So Jaime took Gabby by the arms, as gently as he could while still appearing to be rough to The Stallion. "I will take good care of her, *senor*," he said, donning his best evil smile.

"I'm glad you're willing to soil yourself with this," The Stallion said. "I should have had someone do this long ago. I don't care what you have to do to make her cry. Just do it."

Jaime gave a nod since he didn't trust his voice. He nudged Gabby toward the hallway and she fought him on it, still staring at The Stallion.

"You're a disgusting excuse for a human being. You aren't a human being. You're a monster." And then, apparently taking a page out of Alyssa's book, she spit at him.

The Stallion scrambled away and then furiously scowled at Jaime.

"Are you going to let her get away with that?" he demanded, fury all but pumping out of him.

Oh, damn, Gabby and her mouth. How the hell was he going to get out of this one?

Chapter Eleven

Gabby had gone too far. She realized it a few seconds too late. She'd wanted to make sure The Stallion didn't think she was happy to go with Jaime. She wanted The Stallion to think she hated Jaime as much as she hated him, and she didn't know how to show it considering she didn't hate Jaime even a little bit.

But she'd put Jaime in an impossible position. The Stallion expected Jaime to hurt her now. In front of him.

And how could he not?

Jaime's jaw tightened and Gabby knew it

wasn't because he was getting ready to hurt her. It was because he didn't want to and he was having a hard time figuring out how to avoid it. But he didn't need to protect her.

She lifted her chin, hoping he would understand. "Hit me with your best shot, buddy," she offered.

Much like when he'd come into the room, guns blazing, not using his accent at all, she gave him a little open-eyed glance that she hoped would clue him in.

He had to hit her. There was no choice. She understood that. She wouldn't hold that against him. Besides, he'd pull the punch. It'd be fine.

He raised his hand and she had to close her eyes. She didn't want the image in her head even if she knew he had to do it. She braced herself for the blow, but it never came.

Instead his fingers curled in her hair, a tight

fist. Not comfortable, but still not painful, either.

"It appears you need to be taught some respect, *senorita*. Let's go to your room where I can give you a thorough lesson. I teach best one-on-one."

Gabby opened her eyes, ignoring the shaking in her body. She didn't dare look at The Stallion—she didn't want to know if he'd bought that ridiculous tactic or not. She couldn't look at Jaime, because she didn't want anything to give him or her away.

So she sucked in a breath as though Jaime's fingers in her hair hurt and stared at the floor as if he was forcing her. She stumbled a little as he nudged her forward, trying to make it appear as if he'd pushed her. She put everything into the performance of making it look like he was being rough with her when he was being anything but.

"I will come to give you a full report when I'm done, *senor*."

"Excellent." The Stallion sounded pleased with himself. Satisfied.

Jaime continued to nudge her all the way to her room, and she let out a little squeak of faked pain. When Jaime finally gave her a light push into her room, she could only sag with relief.

Jaime closed the door and flicked the lock. Before she had a moment to breathe, to say a thing, she was being bundled into his arms and gently cradled against his hard chest and the weapons there.

She relaxed into him, letting him hold her up. She was shaking more now, oddly, but it was such an amazing thing to be cradled and comforted after everything that had just happened, she couldn't even wonder over it.

"We need to get you cleaned up," Jaime said, his voice low and sounding pained.

She waved him away, wanting to stay right there, cradled against him. "Leave it. Maybe it'll convince him you were suitably rough with me if we let it bleed more."

"He's not going to see you again," Jaime said fiercely, his arms tightening around her briefly. "You're under lock and key now, and if he tries to come in here, I will kill him myself."

She looked up at him curiously. He was... He'd avoided her for days, and Gabby couldn't blame him because she knew he was trying to do something noble. Still, she didn't quite understand his anger.

Frustration or fear, maybe even annoyance, she might have understood, but the beating fury in his eyes, completely opposite to the gentle way he held her, was something she couldn't unwind.

"What was the other woman's problem?" he asked, studying her nose.

"She hit the two-year mark," Gabby stated with a tired sigh.

"What does that mean?"

Gabby sighed. "Oh, I don't know. It just seems that around two years in here you start to realize how stuck you are. How no one's going to come and save you. I think we all have a little bit of a meltdown at two years."

"Did your two-year meltdown include punching another woman in the face?"

"No. I was alone. I did try to use a butter knife to stab a guard," she offered almost cheerfully.

His mouth almost…almost quirked at that.

"I was desperate," she continued. "With that desperation comes a kind of insanity. Alyssa's hitting that same wall. Losing it. Wondering what it's worth being stuck in this horrible place. Of course, she has the worst possible timing, but what can we do? We just have to try and end it as soon as we can."

"You hugged her." Jaime's voice was soft, awe-filled.

Gabby turned away from him and his comforting, strong arms, uncomfortable with the way he said it as though she'd done something special. But she hadn't. Not really.

"You forget sometimes, when you're in here, that a simple hug can be reassuring. She needed someone to be kind. You...you reminded me of that. Humanity. Compassion. So, I did what you've done to me."

"You did it after she punched you in the nose," he pointed out.

"I let her punch me. I thought it would help her get some of the rage out of her system. I'm hoping getting some of it out will stop her from just...losing it completely."

"You are a marvel," he said, like she was some kind of genius superhero. It shouldn't have warmed her. She should tell him she wasn't.

But she wanted to believe there was something marvelous about her.

"I'm washing you up," he said, taking her arm and pulling her into the little nook that acted as a bathroom. There was a toilet and a sink, but no door, no privacy. Still, Jaime grabbed a washcloth from the little pile she kept neatly stacked in the corner.

He flicked on the tap and soaked the cloth in warm water. He squeezed it out before holding it up to her face gently. Ever so gently, he wiped away the blood that had started dribbling out of her nose after Alyssa had hit her.

"You're lucky she didn't break it," he muttered.

Gabby rolled her eyes. "I *let* her hit me, and

I pulled back a bit. I'm a lot stronger than all that bluster."

He cupped her face with his hands, long fingers brushing at her hairline. "That you are," he said with a kind of fervency that had a lump burning in her throat.

"You've been avoiding me," she rasped.

"Yeah," he said. "I'm trying to do the right thing."

"What about instead of doing the right thing, you do what I want? How about you give me something I want?"

He sighed and shook his head. "I don't know how I ever thought I'd resist you." Then his mouth was on hers.

Potent and hot. Not quite so gentle. Gabby reveled in the fact that he could be both. That he could give her everything and anything she wanted.

"Tell me if I hurt your nose," he murmured

against her mouth, never breaking contact. His hands trailing through her hair, his body pressed hard and tight against hers.

She could barely feel the ache in her nose. Not with Jaime's tongue sliding against hers. Not with the smell of him and leather and what might be outside if she even remembered what outside smelled like.

She realized whatever this was, it was frantic and needy. It was also something that could be temporary all too easily. The chances she'd have to touch him, to be with him…

She needed to grasp and enjoy and lose herself in this moment, in the having of it. She molded her hands against his strong shoulders, slid them down his biceps and his forearms. Everything about him was honed muscle, so strong. He could've been brutal with someone else's heart, but Jaime was anything but that.

His hands smoothed down her neck and, for

the first time, he dared to touch more than just her face or her shoulders. The fingers of one hand traced across her collarbone over her T-shirt. His other hand slid down her back, strong as he held her against him.

She could feel him, hot and hard against her stomach. It had been a long time since she'd done this, and it was possibly the most inappropriate moment, but there wasn't time to think.

She didn't want to think. She wanted to sink into good feelings and let *those* take over for once.

She arched against him and the fingertips tracing her collarbone stilled. Then lowered. He palmed one of her breasts and she moaned against his mouth.

"We can stop whenever," he said, so serious and noble and *wrong*.

"I don't ever want to stop." She wanted to

live in a moment where she had some power. Where she had some hope. "Take off your guns, Jaime."

He stilled briefly and then reached up to the shoulder of the harness and unbuckled it. He pulled the strand of weapons off his body, his eyes never leaving hers. He hesitated only a moment before he laid the weapons down next to her bed.

He took a gun from his waistband she hadn't known was there and placed it on the little table next to her bed. Something almost resembling a smile graced his mouth as he reached to his boots and pulled a knife out of each.

There was something not just weighty about watching him disarm, but something intimate. She watched him strip himself of all the things he used to protect himself. All the things he used to portray another man. To do his job, his duty.

"I think that's all of them," he said in a husky voice.

She didn't have any weapons to surrender, so she grabbed the hem of her shirt and pulled it off. She moved her hands to unbutton her pants, but Jaime made a sound.

"Stop," he ordered.

She raised a questioning eyebrow at him.

He crossed back to her, a hand splaying against her stomach, the other sliding down her arm. "Let me."

She swallowed the nerves fluttering to the surface. No, nerves wasn't the right word. It was something more fundamental than that. Would he like what he saw? Would he still be as enamored with her when they were naked? When it was over?

She wanted to laugh at her momentary worry about such things. But, like so many other thoughts, it was a comforting reaction—a real-life response. That she could still be a woman. That she could still care about such things.

His hands were rough against her skin. Tanned against how pale she was with no access to sunlight. She watched as he traced the strangest parts of her, as if fascinated by her belly button or the curve of her waist. But he was still fully clothed, though he'd surrendered all his weapons.

She gave the hem of his shirt a little tug. "Take this off," she ordered, because it was nice to order. More than nice to have someone obey. Power. Equality, really. He could order her and she could order him, and they could each get what they wanted.

He pulled his shirt off from the back, lifting it over his head and letting it hit the floor. He really was perfection. Tall and lithe and beautiful. He had scars and smooth patches of skin.

Dark hair that drew a line from his chest to the waistband of his jeans.

She moved forward and traced the longest scar on his side. A white line against his golden skin.

"How did you get this?" she asked.

"Knife fight."

She raised her gaze to his eyes, but his expression was serious, not silly. "You were in a *knife* fight?"

He shrugged. "When I first started out as Rodriguez, I was doing some drug running for one of his lower-level operations. Unfortunately a lot of those guys try to double-cross each other. I was caught in the cross…well, cross-stabbing as it were."

He said it so cavalierly, as if that was just part of his job. Getting stabbed. Horribly enough to leave a long, white scar.

"Did you go to the hospital?"

Again he smiled, almost indulgently now. "There was a man who did the stitching back at our home base."

"A man? Not a doctor?" she demanded.

"Doctors were saved from more…life-threatening injuries. Even then, only if you were important. At that point, I wasn't very important."

Gabby tried to make sense of it as Jaime shook his head.

"It's a nonsensical world. None of it makes sense if you have a conscience, if you've known love or joy. Because it's not about anything but greed and power and desperation."

She traced the jagged line and then bent to press a kiss to it. He sucked in a breath.

"I bet there was no one to kiss it better," she said, trying to sound lighthearted even though tears were threatening.

"Ah, no."

"Then let me." She raised to her tiptoes to

kiss him. To press her chest to his. She still wore a bra, but the rest of her upper body was exposed and she tried to press every bare spot of her to every bare spot of him.

She tasted his mouth, his tongue, and she wanted the kiss to go deep enough and mean enough to ease some of those old hurts, some of that old loneliness.

For both of them.

THERE WERE THINGS Jaime should do. Things he should stop from happening. But Gabby's kiss, Gabby's heart, was a balm to all the cruelties he'd suffered and administered in the past two years. She was sweetness and she was light. She was warmth and she was hope.

At this point he could no longer keep it from himself, let alone her. She wanted this. Perhaps she needed it as much as he did. Regardless, there was no going back. There was only going forward.

Her skin was velvet, her mouth honey. Her heart beating against his heart, the cadence of a million wonderful things he'd forgotten existed.

Her fingertips were curious and gentle as they explored him, bold as though it never occurred to her she shouldn't.

All of it was solace wrapped in pleasure and passion. That someone would want to touch him with reverence or care. That he wasn't the hideous monster he'd pretended to be for two years. He was still a man made of flesh and bone, justice and right.

And despite her time here as a victim, she was still a woman. Made of flesh and bone. Made of heart and soul.

He smoothed his hands up and down her

back, absorbing the strength of her. Carefully leashed, carefully honed.

He reached behind her and unsnapped her bra, slowly pulling it off her and down her arms. It meant he had to put space between them. It meant he had to wrestle his mouth from hers. But if anything was worth that separation, it was the sight before him. Gabby's curly hair tumbled around her face. Her lips swollen, her cheeks flushed.

The soft swell of her breasts, dark nipples sharp points because she was as excited as he was. As needy as he was. He palmed both breasts with his too-rough hands and was rewarded by her soft moan.

Of course this amazingly strong and brave woman before him was not content to simply let him look or touch. She reached out and touched him, as well, her hands trailing down his chest all the way to his waistband. She flipped the button and unzipped the piece of clothing with no preamble at all.

He continued to explore her breasts with his hands. Memorizing the weight and the shape and the warmth, the amazing softness her body offered to him. And it was more than just that. So much more than just the body. A heart. A soul. Neither of them would be at this point if it wasn't so much more than *physical*. It was an underlying tie, a cord of inexplicable connection.

She tugged his jeans down, his boxers with them. And then those slim, strong hands were grasping him. Stroking his erection and nearly bringing him to his knees.

He needed to find some sort of center. Not necessarily of control but of reason. Sense and responsibility. This was neither sensible nor responsible, but that didn't mean he couldn't take care of her. That didn't mean he wouldn't.

Gently he pulled her hand off him. "I need to go get something. I'll be right back."

She blinked up at him, eyebrows furrowed. Beautiful and naked from the waist up.

He pressed his mouth to hers as he pulled his jeans up, drowning in it a minute, forgetting what he'd been about to do. It was only when she touched him again that he remembered.

"Stay put. I will be right back." When she opened her mouth, he shook his head. "I promise," he repeated, his gaze steady on hers. He needed her to understand, and he needed her to believe him.

She pouted a little bit, beautiful and sulky, but she nodded.

"Right back," he repeated and then he was rushing to his room, caring far too little about the things he should care about. If The Stallion was around… If the other girls were okay…

But it hardly mattered with Gabby's soul entwined with his.

He went to his closet of a room and grabbed the box that had been given to him. The box was still wrapped and he had no doubt about the safety of its contents.

And he would keep Gabby safe. No matter what.

With a very quick glance toward the back door, Jaime very nearly *scurried* back to Gabby. That back door was clearly shut and locked. Surely The Stallion had disappeared into his lair to obsess over Layne and Wallace's progress.

Jaime entered Gabby's room once again, closing and locking the door behind him quickly. She wasn't standing anymore. She was sitting on the edge of her bed and she was still shirtless.

He walked over and placed the box of condoms on the nightstand next to his smaller gun. He watched her face carefully, something flickering there he didn't recognize as she glanced at the box.

"We still don't have to," he offered, wondering if it was reticence or something close to it.

Her glance flicked from the box to him. "Why do you have these?"

"If you haven't noticed The Stallion is a little convinced women have—"

"Cooties?" Gabby supplied for him.

Jaime laughed. "I was going to say diseases. But, yes, essentially, cooties."

"So he gave those to you?"

"When I convinced him that only female payment would do, he insisted I take the necessary precautions."

She frowned, puzzling over the box. He didn't know what to say to make her okay. But eventually she grabbed the box and ran her nail around the edge. Pulling the wrapping off, she ripped open the box and took out a packet.

She studied him from beneath her lashes and then smirked. "I think this is where you drop your pants."

He laughed again. Laughing. It was amazing considering he couldn't think of the last time he'd laughed. With Gabby he felt like he wasn't just a machine. He wasn't simply a tool to bring The Stallion down or a tool to help The Stallion out. He'd been nothing but a weapon for so long it was hard to remember that he was also real. Capable of laughing. Capable of humor. Capable of feeling.

Capable of caring. Perhaps even loving.

He'd never been a romantic man who believed in flights of fancy and yet this woman had changed his life. She'd changed his heart and he didn't have to know how she'd done it to know that it had happened.

He pushed his jeans the remainder of the way down, watching her the entire time. Her gaze remained bold and appraising on his erection.

She scooted forward on the bed, tearing the condom packet open before rolling it on him. Finally she looked up at him. Her gaze never left his as she lay back on the bed and undid the fastenings of her pants. She shimmied out of her remaining clothes and then lay there, naked and beautiful before him.

He took a minute to drink her in. Because who knew how much time they would have after the next couple of days. He would save her—he would do anything to save her—and he did not know what lay ahead. He did know he had to absorb all of this, commit it to memory, connect it to his heart.

He stepped out of his jeans and then crawled onto the bed and over her. She slid her arms around his neck and pulled his mouth to hers.

The kiss was soft and sweet. An invitation, an enchanting spell.

He traced the curve of her cheek with one hand, positioning himself with the other. Slowly, torturing himself and possibly her, as well, he found her entrance. Nudged against it. Taking his sweet time to slowly enter her.

Joined. Together. As if they were a perfect match. A pair that belonged exactly here. How could he belong anywhere else when this was perfect? When she was perfect?

She arched against him as if hurrying him along, her fingers tightening in his too long hair.

"We have time, Gabby. We have time." He kissed her, soft and sweet, indulging himself in a moment where he was simply seeped inside of her.

A moment when he was all hers and she was all his. And she relaxed, melting. His. All his.

Chapter Twelve

Gabby had known sex with Jaime would be different for a lot of reasons. First and foremost, she wasn't a young girl sneaking around, finding awkward stolen moments in the back of a car. Second, he wasn't a little boy playing at being a hard-ass bad man.

He was a strong, good, *amazing* man, doing things her ex-boyfriend would have wilted in front of.

But mostly, sex with Jaime was different because it was them. Because it was here. Because it mattered in a way her teenage heart would never have been able to understand. Perhaps she never would have been able to understand if she hadn't been in this position. The position that asked her to be more than she'd ever thought she'd be able to be. Because the truth of the matter was, eight years ago she had been a young woman like any other. Selfish and foolish and not strong in the least.

She would never be grateful for this eight years of hell. She would never be happy for the lessons she'd learned here, but that didn't mean she couldn't appreciate them. Because whether she was happy about it or not, it had happened. It was reality. There was only so much bitterness a person could stand.

With Jaime moving inside her, touching her, caring about her, bitterness had no place. Only pleasure. Only hope. Only a deep, abiding care she had never felt before.

He kissed her, soft and gentle, wild and passionate, a million different kinds of kisses and cares. His body moved against hers; rough, strong, such a contrast. Such a perfect fit.

Passion built inside her, deep and abiding. Bigger than anything she'd imagined she'd be able to feel ever again. But Jaime's hands stroked her body. He moved inside her like he could unlock every piece of her. She *wanted* him to.

The blinding spiral of pleasure took her off guard. She hadn't expected it so quickly or so hard. She gasped his name, surprised at the sound in the quiet room. Surprised at all he could draw it out of her.

He still moved with her. Growing a little frantic, a little wild. She reveled in it, her hands sliding down his back. Her heart beating against his.

She wanted *his* release. Wanted to feel him lose himself inside her.

Instead of galloping after it, though, he paused, as if wanting to make this moment last forever. Satisfied and sated, how could she argue with that? She would stay here, locked with him, body to body forever.

He kissed her neck, her jaw. His teeth scraped against her lips and she moved her hips to meet with his. But he was unerringly slow and methodical. As though they'd been making love for years and he knew exactly how to drive her crazy. How to make her fall over that edge again and again. Because she was perilously close.

Aside from the tension in his arms, she would have no idea he was exerting any energy whatsoever. That spurred something in her. Something she hadn't thought she'd ever feel again. A challenge. And need.

She tightened her hold on his shoulders, slicked though they were. She sank her teeth into his bottom lip, pushing hard against him with her hips. He groaned into her mouth. She slid her hands down his back, gripping his hips, urging him on. One hand tightened on her hip, a heavy, hot brand.

She looked into his eyes and smiled at him. "More," she insisted.

He swore, sounding a little broken. That control he'd been holding on to, that calm assault to bring her to the brink, snapped. He moved against her with a wildness she craved, that she reveled in.

She'd brought him to this point, wild and a little broken. *She* could be the woman that did this to him, and that was something no one could ever take away. *She* was the woman who had made him hers. Maybe she wouldn't always have Jaime, but she'd always have this.

He groaned his release, pushing hard against her, and it was the knowledge she'd brought him there that sent her over the edge again herself. Pulsing and crashing. Her heart beating heavy, having grown a million sizes. Having accepted his as her own.

He lay against her, and she stroked her hand up and down his back, listening to his heart beat slowly, slowly, come back to its regular rhythm. He made a move to get off her, but she held him there, wanting his weight on her for as long as it could be.

"Aren't I crushing you?" he asked in her ear, his voice a low rumble.

"I like it," she murmured in return.

He nuzzled into her neck, relaxing into her. As though because she'd said she liked it he would give her this closeness for as long as he could. She believed that about him. That he would always give her whatever he could. Once they knew Natalie was safe, he'd agreed to get her out under any means possible, and she believed.

For the first time in eight years she believed in someone aside from herself. For the first time in eight years she had hope and care and pleasure.

She might've told him she loved him in any other situation, but this was no regular life. Love was… Who knew what love really was? If they got away, back into the real world, maybe…maybe she could learn.

JAIME SLEPT IN Gabby's bed. It was a calculated risk to spend the night with her. He didn't know how close an eye The Stallion was keeping on him with everything going on. In the end, perhaps a little addled by her and sex, he'd figured, if pressed, he'd explain all his time as making sure Gabby paid for her supposed lack of respect.

It bothered him to have to think of things like that. Bothered him in a way nothing in the past two years had. That he had to make The Stallion think he was hurting Gabby. It grated against every inch of him every time he thought about it.

So he tried not to think about it. He spent the night in her bed and the next day mostly holed up with her in her room. They made love. They talked. They *laughed*.

It felt as though they were anywhere but in this prison. A vacation of sorts. Just one where you didn't leave the room you were locked into. He wouldn't regret this time. It was something to have her here, to have her close.

They didn't talk about the future or about what they might do when they got out. Jaime would have some compulsory therapy to go through. A whole detox situation with the FBI, along with preparations for the future trial.

Any further investigating that needed to be done would at least fall somewhat within his responsibility.

But he was done with undercover work. He'd known that before he'd met Gabby. These past two years had taken too much of a toll and he couldn't be a good law-enforcement officer in this position anymore. He didn't plan to leave the FBI, but undercover work was over.

Once he got Gabby out, he would make sure that "something different" included her. She would need therapy, as well, and time to heal. It would take time to find ways back to their old selves.

He could wait. He could do anything if it meant having a chance with her.

But their time here in this other world was running out. The Stallion would be expecting a full report from Rodriguez, and Jaime had put it off long enough.

He would do all the things he had to do to protect her. To free her.

"You have to go meet with him," she said, her tone void of any emotion.

He turned to face her on the bed. It was too narrow and they barely fit together, and yet he was grateful for the lack of space, for the excuse to always be this close. "How'd you figure that out?"

"You got all tense," she replied, rubbing at his shoulders as though this was something they could be. A couple. Who talked to each other, offered comfort to each other.

He couldn't think of anything he'd ever wanted more, including his position with the FBI.

"He's expecting a report from me."

Gabby frowned and didn't look at him when she asked her question. "Are you going to tell him I cried?"

He'd been planning on it. He knew it poked her pride, but it would be best if The Stallion thought her broken. It would be best if Jaime made himself look like a master torturer.

"Do you not want me to?"

"You would tell him you failed?"

He shrugged, trying to act as though it wasn't a big deal, though it was. "If you want me to. I don't think it would put me in any danger to make it look like I'd failed one thing considering everything else that's currently going down."

"You don't *think*?"

"He's not exactly the most predictable man in the world, no matter how scheduled and regimented he is."

"That's very true," she mused, looking somewhere beyond him.

"Gabby."

Her dark gaze met his, that warrior battle

light in them. "Tell him I cried. Tell him I sobbed and begged. What does it matter? I didn't actually."

"If it matters something to you—"

"All that matters to me is you." She blinked as if surprised by the force of her words. "And getting out of here," she added somewhat after the fact.

He pressed a kiss to her mouth. Whatever tension he'd had was gone. Or perhaps not *gone*, but different somehow.

Screw The Stallion. Screw responsibility. She was all that mattered. He wanted to believe that as he fell into the kiss, wanted to hold on to that possibility, that new tenet of his life. Gabby and only Gabby.

But life was never quite that easy. Because Gabby, being the most important thing, the central thing for him, meant he had to keep her safe. It meant that responsibility *did* have a place here. It was his responsibility to get her out. His responsibility to get her *free*.

He started to pull away but she spoke before he could.

"Go have a meeting. Find out if there's any news about Nattie, and make sure you re-member every last detail. And then, when you can…" She smoothed her hand over his chest and offered him a smile that was weak at best, but she was trying. For him, he knew.

"When you're done, when you can, come back to me," she said softly.

He brought her hand to his mouth and pressed a kiss to her palm. "Always," he said, holding her gaze. Hoping she understood and believed how much he meant that.

He slid out of bed, because the sooner he got this meeting with The Stallion over with, the sooner he could find a way to make sure that this was over. For Gabby and for him.

Jaime collected his weapons. He could feel Gabby's eyes on him though he couldn't read her expression. She had perfected the art of giving nothing away and as much as it sometimes frustrated him as a man, he was certainly glad she had built such effective protective layers for herself.

He put the knives back in his boots and then strapped on his cross-chest holster with all of his guns. He buckled it, still watching her expressionless face.

She slid off the bed and crossed to him. She flashed a smile Jaime didn't think had much happiness behind it, but she brushed her lips against his.

"Good luck," she said as though she were scared. For him.

"I have to lock the door," he said, regretting the words as they came out of his mouth. Regretting the way her expression shuttered.

"Yeah, I know." She gave a careless shrug.

Her knowing didn't make him feel any better about doing it, but he had to. There were certain things he still had to do. Things that would keep her safe in the end, and that was all that could matter.

He kissed her once more, knowing he was only delaying the inevitable. He steeled all that certainty and finally managed to back himself out of the room. Away from her smile, away from her sweet mouth.

Away from his heart and soul.

He closed the door and locked it from the outside. He regretted having to add the chain, but any regrets were a small price to pay to get her out. He would keep telling himself that over and over again until he believed it. This was all a small price to pay for getting her out.

He walked briskly down the hall, noting the house was eerily quiet. It wasn't unusual, but often in the afternoon there was a little bit of chatter from the common rooms as the girls worked on their projects or fixed dinner.

Jaime cursed and retraced his steps to check on them. The two calm ones from yesterday were sitting on the couch working on something The Stallion had undoubtedly given them to do. Alyssa was pacing the kitchen.

None of them looked at him, so he could only assume he'd been quiet enough. Satisfied that things seemed to be mostly normal, he backed out of the room. Alyssa's frenzied pacing bothered him a bit. Gabby was right, the girl was a loose cannon, and it was the last thing they needed. But what could he do about it?

There wasn't anything. Not now.

He walked back along the hallway, going through the hassle of unlocking and unchaining the door, stepping out, then redoing all the work. His thoughts were jumbled and he had to sort them out before he actually saw The Stallion.

He paused in the backyard, taking a deep breath, trying to focus his thoughts. He forced himself to hone in on all the strategies he'd been taught in his years as a police officer and FBI agent.

He had to put on the cloak of Rodriguez, get the information he was after, lie to The Stallion about Gabby, then go back to her. Once this was over, he could go back to her.

With a nod to himself, he stepped forward, but it was then he heard the noise. Something strange and faint. Almost a moan. He paused and studied the yard around him.

The next sound wasn't so much a moaning but almost like someone rasping "Rodriguez" and failing.

Jaime started moving toward the noise, listening hard as he walked around the backyard.

He held his small handgun in one hand, leaving his other hand free should he need to fight off any attacker.

He rounded the front of the house, still listening to the sound and following the source. When he did, he nearly gasped.

Wallace and Layne were sprawled out in the yard. Layne was a little closer to the house than Wallace, but they were both caked with blood and dirt.

"Rodriguez. Rodriguez." Layne moved his arm wildly and stumbled to his feet. "I've been dragging this piece of shit for who knows how long. Go get The Stallion. And water. By God, I need water."

"Where is your vehicle?" Jaime asked, his tone dispassionate and unhurried.

"Only go so far…" Layne gasped for air, stumbling to the ground again. "Asshole shot our tires. Got as far as I could."

Jaime looked at both men in various states of bloodied harm. "You don't have her."

Layne's dirty, bloody face curled into a scowl, but he gave brief shake of the head.

"I don't know if you want me to get The Stallion if you don't have her."

"He shot us," Layne said disgustedly. "That prick shot us. Wallace might die. We need The Stallion. We need *help*."

"You may wish you had died," Jaime said, affecting as much detached disinterest as he could.

On the inside he was reeling. Gabby's sister had escaped these men with Ranger Cooper, which meant that it was time. It was time to move forward. It was time to get the hell out. Her sister was safe and now it was her turn.

"Go get The Stallion," Layne yelled, lunging at him. He had a bloody wound on his shoulder and he was pale. Still, he seemed to be in slightly better shape than Wallace who was lying on the ground moaning, a bullet wound apparently in his thigh.

After a long study that had Layne growling at him as he tried to walk farther, Jaime inclined his head and then began striding purposefully back to The Stallion's shed. He knocked and only entered once The Stallion unlocked the door and bid him entrance.

"What took you so long?" The Stallion demanded and Jaime was more than a little happy that he had a decent enough excuse to explain his long absence in a way that didn't have anything to do with Gabby.

"*Senor*, Wallace and Layne are in the yard. Injured."

The Stallion had just sat in his desk chair, but immediately leaped to his feet. "They don't have her?" he bellowed.

"No."

"Imbeciles. Useless, worthless trash. Kill them. Kill them both immediately," he ordered with the flick of a wrist.

Jaime had to curb his initial reaction, which was to refuse. He might find Wallace and Layne disgusting excuses for human beings, he might even believe they deserved to die, but he was not comfortable with it being at his hand.

"*Senor*, if this is your wish, I will absolutely mete out your justice. But perhaps…"

"Perhaps what?" he snapped.

"You will want to go after the girl yourself, *sí*?"

The Stallion frowned as he walked over and stood by his dolls, grabbing one hand as though he was holding the hand of a little girl.

Jaime had to ignore that and press his advantage. "Clearly the Ranger is smarter than your men. But certainly not smarter than you. If you go after him, you can do whatever you want with both of them. Surely you, of all people, could outsmart them."

The Stallion had begun to nod the more Jaime complimented him. "You're right. You're right."

He dropped the doll's hand and Jaime nearly sagged with relief.

"You'll have to go with me, Rodriguez."

Jaime stilled. That was not part of his plan. "Tell Layne and Wallace they're in charge of the girls. We'll leave immediately."

"Their injuries are severe. Shot. Both of them. Surely incapable of watching after anything. You must have other men you can take with you, and I'll stay—"

"No." The Stallion shook his head. "No, you're coming with me. Wallace and Layne, no matter how injured, can keep a door locked. I'll send for another man, and he can kill them and take over here. Yes, yes, that's the plan. I need you. I need you, Rodriguez." The Stallion took one of the dolls off the shelf. He petted the doll's dark hair as though it were a puppy. "If you prove your worth to me on this, there is nothing that I wouldn't give you, Rodriguez." He held out the doll between them.

Jaime was afraid he looked as horrified as he felt, but he kept his hands grasped lightly behind his back. He forced himself to smile languidly at the unseeing doll. "Then I am at your service, *senor.*"

"Go tell them the plan," The Stallion said, gesturing with the doll, thank God not making him take it. "Not the killing part, of course, just the watching-after-the-girls part. Pack all your weapons and all your ammunition. Pack up all the water in my supplies and put it in the Jeep. We'll leave as soon as you've gotten everything together. Do you understand?"

Jaime nodded, trying to steady the panic rising inside him. *"Sí, senor."*

It wasn't such a terrible thing. He'd be there to stop The Stallion from getting any kind of hold on Gabby's sister and Ranger Cooper. But it left Gabby here. Exposed.

And he only had limited time to figure out how to fix that.

Chapter Thirteen

Gabby tried to ignore how locked in she felt. She'd been a victim for eight years. A prisoner of this place. Being locked in her room and unable to leave was certainly no greater trial to bear.

But she hadn't been locked in her room for any stretch of time since the very beginning. Mostly she'd been able to go to the common room or the kitchen whenever she wanted.

She'd gotten used to that freedom, and it was clawing at her to have lost some of it. That made it a very effective punishment all in all.

She wondered what the girls were doing. Had Alyssa calmed down? Was she ranting? Was she bringing reality to her threat to kill everyone in an effort to get out of there?

Gabby buried her face in her pillow and tried to block it all out, but when she inhaled she could smell Jaime and something in her chest turned over.

Oh, Jaime. That was part of why this locked-up thing was harder to bear, too. She'd felt almost real for nearly twenty-four hours. She and Jaime had spent the night, and most of today, having sex and talking and enjoying each other's company. As though they lived in an outside world where they were themselves and not undercover agent and kidnapping victim.

It made it so much harder to be fully forced into what she really was. Victim. Captive. Not any closer to having any power than she'd been twenty-four hours ago.

Except she'd stolen a moment of it, and wasn't that something worth celebrating?

She heard someone unlocking her door from the outside and sat bolt upright in bed. Jaime hadn't been gone very long. If he was back already, it had to be bad news.

If it wasn't Jaime on the other side, so much the worse.

But it was the man she'd taken as a lover who stepped into her room, shutting the door behind him with more force than necessary. His face reminded her of that first day. Rodriguez. The mask, not the man.

"Do you have anything in here you'd want to take with you?" he demanded.

"What?" She couldn't follow him as he walked the perimeter of her room as if searching for something valuable.

"I don't have time to explain. I don't have time to do anything but get you out now."

"What happened?" she asked, jumping off the bed.

His hand curled around her forearm, tight and without any of its usual kindness. "Is there anything you need to take?" he repeated, glaring at her.

"What's happened?" she pleaded with him. Her heart beat a heavy cadence against her chest and she couldn't think past the panic gripping her. "Is it Nattie? Is—"

He began pulling her to the door. "Your sister and the Ranger escaped."

"Escaped? Escaped!" Hope burst in her chest, bright and wonderful. "So we're…we're just running?"

He looked up and down the hallway. "You are. I'll get the other girls after."

That stopped Gabby in her tracks, no matter how he pulled on her arm. "What?" she demanded.

"Layne and Wallace are hurt. I can get one of you out now without raising any questions because you're supposed to be locked up, but I can't get you all out. Not right this second. I have to go with The Stallion to track down your sister. Which is good," he said before she could argue with him or ask him what the hell he was talking about. "Because I will obviously make sure that doesn't happen. I have—" he glanced at his watch "—maybe five seconds to contact my superiors to let them know to raid this place, and then to try to find one just like it in the south." He shoved her into the hallway, but she fought him.

"You can't take me and not them."

His gaze locked on hers. "Of course I can. And that's what we're doing."

"No. You can't. They'll fall apart without me."

"They won't. And they'll be saved in a day or two. Three tops."

"You really expect me to leave Tabitha and Jasmine here with Alyssa? Alyssa will instigate something. You know she will. They'll all be dead before..." She didn't want to say it out loud, no matter how much he wasn't being careful himself.

He grabbed her by the shoulders and gave her a little shake, his eyes fierce and stubborn. "But you won't be."

It was her turn to look up and down the hallway. She didn't know where the girls were, where Wallace and Layne or The Stallion were milling about. Jaime was losing his mind and it was her... Well, it was her responsibility to make him find it.

"You have to get it together," she snapped in a low, quiet voice. "You have to be sensible about this, and you have to calm down."

He thrust his fingers into his hair, looking more than a little wild. "Gabby, I do not have time. You have to do what I say, and you have to do it now."

"Take Alyssa," she said, though it pained her to offer that. A stabbing pain of fear, but it was the only option.

"Wh-what?" he spluttered.

"Take Alyssa. I can handle more days here. Tabitha and Jasmine… We can hack it, but Alyssa cannot take another day. You know that. Take her. Get her out, we'll cover it up, and when the raid comes, you will come and get me."

"Have you lost your mind?"

"No! You've lost yours." Part of her wanted to push him, or reverse their positions and shake him, but the bigger part of her wanted to reach something in him. She curled her fingers into his shirt. "You know it isn't safe to take me out. Why are you risking everything?"

"Because I love you," he blurted, clearly antagonized into the admission.

She only stared up at him. It wasn't… She… Love.

"I do not have time to argue," he said, low and fierce.

That, she was sure, was absolutely true. He didn't have time to argue. He didn't have time to think. But she knew the girls better than he did. She knew…

She reached her hands up and cupped his face. She drew strength from that. From him. From love. "If you love me," she said, low and in her own kind of fierce, "then understand that I know what they can handle. What they can't. I couldn't live with myself if I got out and they didn't. Not like this."

She wasn't sure what changed in him. There was still an inhuman tenseness to his muscles and yet some of that fierceness in him had dimmed.

"What am I supposed to do if something happens to you?" he asked, his voice pained and gravelly.

"I can take care of myself." She knew it wasn't totally true. A million things could go wrong, but she had to trust him to leave and save Nattie, and he needed to trust her to stay and keep the girls alive.

That she'd have a much easier time of doing if he took Alyssa. No matter that it made her want to cry. No matter that she wanted to be selfish and take the spot. But she couldn't imagine living the rest of her life if their deaths were on her head.

If there was a chance to get them *all* out, alive and safe, she had to take it. Not the one that only saved her. "You know I'm right."

He looked away from her, though his tight

grip on her shoulders never loosened. "You understand that I have to go. I don't have a choice."

"I want you to go. To save my sister."

His gaze returned to hers, flat and hard. "I'm not taking Alyssa."

"What? You have to." She gripped his shirt harder in an attempt to shake him. "If you can get one of us—"

"Gabby, I could get you out. Because you're supposed to be locked up, but more because I know you could do it. I could trust you to handle anything that came our way. I can't trust Alyssa. I can't trust her to keep her mouth shut when it counts. I can't trust her to get home. Like you said, she can't hack it. If I can't leave her here, then I can't take her, either."

"Then take one of the other girls!"

"You said it yourself. Alyssa would blab someone was missing. She'd… You can't trust

her not to get you all killed. Don't you understand? It's you or no one."

"Why are you doing this?" she demanded,
tears flooding her eyes. It wasn't fair. It wasn't
right. He should take someone. Someone had
to survive this.

"I'm not doing anything. I saw a chance for
you—you, Gabby, to escape. If you won't take
it, there's no substitute here. There is only you
or nothing."

"Why are you trying to manipulate me into
this? If you love me—"

"Why are you trying to manipulate my love?
I know what the hell I'm doing, too. I have
been trained for this. I have—"

"Gabby?"

Gabby and Jaime both jerked, looking down
the hallway to Jasmine standing wide-eyed at
the end of it. "What's going on?"

Jaime shook his head. "I can't do this. I don't

have time to do this." Completely ignoring Jasmine, he got all up in Gabby's face, pulling her even closer, his dark eyes blazing into her. "I can save you *now*, but you have to come with me now. This is your last chance."

"It's your last chance to think reasonably," she retorted.

He looked to the ceiling and inhaled before crushing his mouth to hers, as though Jasmine wasn't standing right there. He seemed to pour all his frustration and all his fear into the kiss, and all Gabby could do was accept it.

"Goodbye, Gabby," he said on a ragged whisper, releasing her. "I love you, and I will get you safe."

She started to say his name as he walked away, but stopped herself as she looked at Jasmine. She couldn't say his real name. Even if she trusted Jasmine, she couldn't… This was all too dangerous now.

She wanted to tell him to save her sister. She wanted to tell him she loved him. She wanted to tell him he was being unfair and wrong, and yet none of those words poured out as he started to walk away. She wanted to tell him to be safe. That it would kill her if he was hurt.

But Jasmine was watching and she had to let him walk away. To save her sister. To save them all.

"What's happening?" Jasmine asked in a shaky voice. "I don't understand anything that I just saw."

Gabby slumped against the wall. "I don't know. I don't…"

"Yes, you do," Jasmine snapped, her voice sharp and uncompromising.

Gabby felt the tears spill unbidden down her cheeks. What was happening? She didn't understand any of it. But she knew she had to be strong. If they were going to be saved, she had to be strong.

She reached out for Jasmine, gratified when the girl offered support.

"We need to make a plan," Gabby said, sounding a lot stronger than she felt.

JAIME WASN'T SURE he could hide his dark mood if he tried. He was furious. Furious with Gabby for not coming with him. Furious at The Stallion for being the kind of fool who needed him to be there to do all the dirty work. Furious at the world for giving him something beautiful and then taking it all away.

Or are you just terrified?

He ground his teeth together and slid a look at The Stallion. The man sat in the passenger seat of the Jeep, typing on his laptop, swearing every time his Wi-Fi hotspot lost any kind of signal. He had a tricked-out assault rifle sitting precariously on his lap.

Jaime drove fueled on fear and anger. He'd had to leave the compound before he'd been able to be certain his message to his superiors had gone through. For all he knew, he could be out there alone with no backup. Gabby could be alone with no backup.

He wanted to rage. Instead he drove.

They were in the Guadalupe Mountains now, having driven through the night. Apparently, Gabby's sister and Ranger Cooper had run this way. Jaime was skeptical, considering how isolated it was. How would they be surviving?

But it didn't really matter. If they were on the wrong track, all the better.

What would actually be all the better would be reaching down to his side piece and ending this once and for all. It would put an end to two years of suffering. Eight for Gabby. Who knew how much suffering for everyone else.

But no matter how much anger and fury pumped through his veins, he knew he couldn't do it. Those same people who had been victims deserved answers and they deserved justice. In an operation like The Stallion's, so big, so vast, taking the big man out would produce perhaps a confused few days, but someone would quickly and easily usurp that power. Taking over as if The Stallion had never existed. It would create even more victims than already existed.

He couldn't overlook that. His duty was his duty. Intractable no matter how unfair it seemed. No matter what Gabby would think of it.

Gabby had implored him to trust her and, in the moment, he hadn't. He'd been too blinded by his fear and his anger that she wouldn't go with him.

In the quiet of driving through these deserted mountains, Jaime could only relive that moment. Over and over again. Regret slicing through him. He'd ended things so badly, and there was such a chance—

No. He wouldn't let himself think that way. There was no chance he wouldn't see Gabby again. No good chance they didn't escape this. He would find a way and so would she.

"Drive up there." The Stallion pointing at, what seemed to Jaime, a random mountain.

"There is no road."

The Stallion gave him a doleful look. "Drive to the top of that mountain," he repeated.

Jaime inclined his head. *"Sí, senor."* He drove, adrenaline pumping too hard as the Jeep skidded and halted up the rocky incline. He gripped the wheel, tapping the brakes, doing everything he could to remain in control of the vehicle.

Finally, The Stallion instructed him to stop. The man pulled out a pair of high-tech binoculars and began to search the horizon.

Jaime watched the man. He looked like any man, hunting or perhaps watching birds. He appeared completely sane and normal, and yet Jaime had seen him fondle dolls like they were real people.

"*Senor*, may I ask you a question?" It was a dangerous road to take. If The Stallion read anything suspicious into his questioning, Jaime could end up dead in the middle of this mountainous desert.

But The Stallion nodded regally as if granting an audience with the peasants.

"If you believe women are diseased, so you say, why do you keep so many of them?"

The Stallion seemed to ponder the line of

questioning. Eventually he shrugged. "Waste not, want not."

Jaime didn't have to feign a language barrier for that to not make sense at all. "I… Come again?"

"Waste not, want not," The Stallion repeated. "I find them hideous creatures myself, as the perfect woman remains elusive. But some men, like yourself, require certain payments. Why should I waste the work they can do for the possible insurance they can offer me? It only makes sense to keep them. To use them. In fact, it's what women were really meant for. To be used. Perhaps the perfect woman is just a myth. And my mother was a dirty liar." The Stallion's fingers tightened on his gun, though he still held the binoculars with his other hand.

Jaime said nothing more. It was best if he stopped asking for motives and started focusing on what he was going to do if they found

Natalie and Ranger Cooper. Focus on thwarting The Stallion's plans without tipping him off to it.

Or you could just kill him.

It was so tempting, Jaime found his hand drifting down to the piece on his left side without really thinking about it.

"There!" The Stallion shouted, pointing.

Jaime blinked down at the bright desert and mountain before them.

"I saw something down there. Get out of the Jeep. Remember, I don't care what happens to the Ranger, but I want the girl alive."

The Stallion jumped out of the Jeep, scrambling over the loose rock, his gun cocked, laptop and binoculars forgotten in the passenger seat.

Though Jaime wanted nothing to do with this, he also jumped out of the car. He had to make sure The Stallion did nothing to Ranger Cooper or Gabby's sister.

Jaime grabbed a gun for each hand. It was easy to catch up with The Stallion given Jaime's legs were longer. Since The Stallion had his gun raised to his shoulder, Jaime pretended to accidentally skid into him as he fired his weapon.

"Damn it, Rodriguez. I had a shot!" The Stallion bellowed.

Jaime surveyed the ground below. He could see two figures standing like sitting ducks in the middle of the desert. They were too far away to make a shot a sure thing, but why weren't they moving after that first shot?

Jaime raised his gun. "Allow me, *senor*."

Jaime was surprised that his arm very nearly shook as he took aim. He'd used his guns plenty in the past two years, though usually to disarm someone or to scare them, not to kill them.

This was no different. He aimed as close as he could without risking any harm and fired.

"You idiot!"

"They are too far away. We have to be closer."

"Like hell." The Stallion raised his gun again and since Jaime couldn't run into him again, he did the only other thing he could think of. He sneezed, loudly.

Again, The Stallion's shot went wide. He snapped his furious gaze on Jaime, and as his head and body turned toward him, so did the gun.

Jaime held himself unnaturally still, doing everything he could to show no fear or reaction to that gun pointed in his direction. He couldn't clear his throat to speak, and he could barely hear his own thoughts over the beating of his heart.

"*Perdón, senor*, but we need to be closer," Jaime said as if a gun that could blow him to pieces wasn't very nearly trained on him at close range. "If you want to ensure the Ranger is dead and the girl is yours, we need to be closer." Jaime pointed out over the desert below, where the couple was now running.

With no warning, The Stallion jerked the gun their way and shot. The woman scrambled behind the outcropping, but Jaime watched as Ranger Cooper jerked. Jaime winced, but Cooper didn't fall. He kept running. Until he was behind the rock outcropping with Gabby's sister.

"Get in the Jeep," The Stallion ordered with calm and ruthless efficiency, making Jaime wonder if he was really crazy at all.

Jaime nodded, knowing he was on incredibly thin ice. The Stallion could shoot him at any time.

You could shoot him first.

He could. God, he could all but feel himself doing it, but Gabby was back in that compound, defenseless. And if the message hadn't gotten through to his superiors… Even if he shot The Stallion his cover would be blown. He'd have to take Ranger Cooper back, and the FBI would intercept all that. Then they'd make him follow their rules and regulations to get Gabby out.

As long as he remained Rodriguez, there was a chance to get Gabby, and the rest of the girls, out by any means necessary.

So he drove the Jeep like a madman down to where the couple had been hiding.

"They are gone by now," Jaime said, perhaps a little too hopefully.

"Keep driving. Find them." The Stallion clenched and unclenched his hand on the rifle.

Jaime did as he was told, driving around mountains until The Stallion told him to stop.

"Stay in the Jeep," The Stallion ordered. "Turn off the ignition. When I call for you, you run. Do you *comprende*?"

Jaime nodded and The Stallion got out of the Jeep, striding away. Jaime thought about staying put for all of five seconds and then he set out to follow his enemy.

Chapter Fourteen

Gabby sat in the common room with Jasmine, Tabitha and Alyssa. They were huddled on the couch, pretending to work on a project The Stallion had given them a few days ago. Layne and Wallace were groaning and limping around the house. Both clearly very injured and yet not seeking any medical attention.

"They're vulnerable. We have to press our advantage now. We have to hit them where it hurts," Alyssa whispered fiercely, staring daggers at the men who were currently groaning about in the kitchen.

Jasmine looked down at her lap, pale and clearly not wanting any part of this powwow, but...

"Unfortunately she's right," Gabby said. "It's our only chance. They've had time to call for backup. The longer we wait...the more chance someone else comes."

She felt guilty for not telling them about the possibility of an FBI raid. They deserved to know the full truth, and they deserved to know what possibilities lay ahead, but Gabby knew they had to get Alyssa out of there before she got killed or got them all killed. They couldn't wait for the FBI to come. They couldn't wait for Jaime to magically fix everything.

No, they had to act.

"We have to time it exactly and precisely. Two of us against one, the other two against the other. Same time. Same attack. Same plan."

Gabby took stock of the two men grousing

in the kitchen then of the three women huddled around her. Alyssa practically jumped out of her seat, completely ready to go, Tabitha looked grim and certain, but Jasmine looked pale and scared.

Gabby didn't want to draw attention to that. Not with Alyssa as…well, whatever Alyssa was. Without looking at her, Gabby reached over and gave Jasmine's hand a squeeze.

"I'm just not strong like you, Gabby," she whispered. "What if I mess up?"

Alyssa started to say something harsh but Gabby stopped her with a look. "That's why we're doing it in pairs. We're a team. Me and Jasmine. Alyssa and Tabitha. Right?"

Alyssa mostly just swore and Gabby watched her carefully. Jaime's words about trusting her rang through her head. Because how could she trust a woman who'd clearly lost her mind? Who'd just as soon kill them all as anything else?

But Jaime had been too cautious. Too afraid for her safety. Gabby didn't have anyone's safety to be afraid for right now. She and the girls were getting to the now-or-never point. Alyssa was already there, and though Tabitha and Jasmine had been somewhat more resilient, they had to feel as she did. They had to be losing that perilous grip on who they were.

Jaime had given herself back to her. Hope, a possible future, but those women hadn't had that. So she had to get them free.

"We'll take Layne," Gabby said, nudging Jasmine with her shoulder. "You two will have Wallace."

"But he's the bigger one," Jasmine whispered.

"It'll be fine. He has a gunshot wound to the

shoulder. Wallace has one to the leg. We're four healthy, capable women."

"B-but what do we do, exactly? After we attack them, what do we do? Run?" Tabitha asked, clearly forcing herself to be strong.

"Kill them. We want to kill them. They did this to us. They deserve to die," Alyssa all but chanted, a wild gleam to her eyes.

Gabby wasn't sure why she hesitated at that. She had indeed been stripped from her life by men like these two, and they surely deserved death. But she found she didn't want to be the one to give it to them.

"We're going to use their injuries to our advantage, hurt them, and then tie them up so we can get away without fear of being followed."

Alyssa scoffed. "I'm going to kill him."

Gabby reached over and grabbed Alyssa's hands, trying to catch her frenzied gaze. "Please. Understand. I don't want to be haunted by this for the rest of my life. I want to leave here and leave it *behind*. No killing unless we absolutely have to. If we have a hope of getting out of here as unharmed as we are in *this* moment, we don't kill them. We incapacitate them."

"And then what? We're just going to run? Run where?"

"I have a vague notion of where we are, and that will help get us out. We've survived this, we can survive walking until we find a town."

Alyssa shook her head in disgust, but Gabby squeezed her hands tighter.

"I need you with me on this. We need to all be together and on the same page. Don't you want to be able to go home and go back to your old life and not have that on your conscience?"

"Who said I have a conscience?" Alyssa retorted, and for a very quick second Gabby believed her, believed that coldness. She'd seen nothing but cold for eight years.

Until Jaime.

That made Gabby fight so much harder. "The four of us are in this together. The four of us. They can't take that away from us. We have survived together, and when we get out, we will still be indelibly linked by that. We're like sisters. They can't make us turn on each other. You can't let them. As long as we work together, as long as we're linked, they can't hurt us."

Gabby wasn't certain that was true. They had guns and weapons, after all. But they were hurt. She had to believe it gave her and the girls an advantage.

Alyssa was looking at her strangely. "Sisters," she whispered. "I don't… No one's ever fought with me before."

"We will," Tabitha said, adding her hand

to Gabby's on top of Alyssa's. Then Jasmine added her hand.

"We don't get out of this without each other," Gabby said, glancing back at Wallace and Layne. Wallace was still moaning, but Layne was glancing their way.

"We'll slowly make excuses to go to our rooms, but you'll all come to mine," she whispered as she pulled her hand from the girls.

Jasmine brought her sewing back to her lap and Tabitha pretended to examine the next package they were supposed to hide in the stuffing of a toy dog.

Gabby got to her feet, but Layne was there and, with his good arm, he shoved her back down.

Well, crap. This wasn't going to go well.

"Problem?" she asked sweetly, looking up at his suspicious gaze. She probably should avert her gaze and show some sort of deference to the man with a gun in his waistband and a nasty expression on his face.

"Aren't you supposed to be locked up?"

"I was just going back to my room when you shoved me back to the couch so rudely."

"I'd watch how you talk to me, little girl," Layne seethed, getting his face into hers.

Gabby bit her tongue because what she really wanted to do was tell *him* to be careful how he talked to her, and then punch him in his bloody bandage as hard and painfully as she could.

Instead she slowly got to her feet, unfolding to her full height. Though he was still much taller than she was, she affected her most condescending stare, never breaking eye contact with him as she stood there, shoulders back.

She was more than a little gratified by the way he seemed to wilt just a teeny tiny bit. As if he knew he couldn't break her.

"I'll just be going to my room now. Feel free to lock my door behind me."

"You little—" He lifted his meaty hand, she supposed to backhand her, and she probably should have let him hit her. She probably should let this all go, but whatever instincts to defend herself she'd tried to eradicate surged to life. She grabbed his hand before it could land across her face, and then put all her force behind shoving him, trying to make contact with his injury.

He stumbled back, though he didn't fall. He let out a hideous moan as, with his bad arm, he pulled the gun from his waistband and trained it on Gabby.

She was certain she was dead. She stood there, waiting for the firearm to go off. Waiting for the piercing pain of a bullet. Or maybe she wouldn't feel it at all. Maybe she would simply die.

But before another breath could be taken, Alyssa was in front of her, and then Tabitha and Jasmine at her sides.

"You'll have to get through us to shoot her, and if you shoot all of us?" Alyssa pretended to ponder that. "I doubt The Stallion would be too pleased with you."

"I'll kill all of you without breaking a sweat, you miserable—"

"Isn't it cute?" Alyssa said, looking back at Gabby. "He thinks *he's* in charge, not his exacting, demanding boss. Well, I guess it takes some balls to be that stupid."

Gabby closed her eyes, she didn't think goading him was really the road to take here, but he hadn't fired.

Yet.

There was a quiet standoff and Gabby tried to rein in the heavy overbeating of her heart. Jasmine's hand slid into hers and Tabitha's arm wound around her shoulders. Alyssa faced off with Layne as if she had no fear whatsoever.

Together, they couldn't be hurt. God, she very nearly believed it.

"If you aren't in your rooms in five seconds, I will shoot all of you," Layne said menacingly.

Gabby didn't believe him, but she didn't want to risk it, either. The girls in front of her hurried down the hall first, and Gabby tried to follow, but Layne grabbed her arm as she passed, digging his heavy fingers into her skin hard enough to leave bruises.

"Tonight you'll be screaming my name," he hissed.

Gabby smiled. It was either that or throw up. "Maybe you'll be screaming mine." She yanked her arm out of his grasp.

She was pretty sure the only thing that kept Layne from shooting her at this point was Wallace's sharp stand-down order.

When Gabby got to her room, she locked the door behind her. It wouldn't keep her safe from Layne since he undoubtedly had a key, but it at least gave her the illusion of safety.

When she turned back to face her room, the girls were all there, Tabitha and Jasmine on her bed, Alyssa pacing the room.

"And now we plan," Alyssa said, that dark glint in her eyes comforting for the first time.

JAIME STALKED THE STALLION. It wasn't easy to carefully follow a man who was carefully following another man, especially through a weirdly arid desert landscape dotted by mountains and rock outcroppings. But then, when had any of this been *easy*?

The Stallion stopped as though he'd seen something, and Jaime waited a beat. He realized The Stallion was peering around a swell of earth, and when The Stallion didn't move forward in the swiftly calculating pace he'd been employing, Jaime sucked in a breath.

On a hunch and a prayer, Jaime snuck around the other side of it. He kept his footsteps slow and quiet.

And then a shot rang out.

Jaime took off in a run, skidding to a halt when he saw The Stallion and Ranger Cooper standing off.

Jaime couldn't hear their conversation, but both men were unharmed and The Stallion didn't fire. Jaime dropped the small handguns he'd been carrying for ease of movement and unholstered his largest and most accurate weapon.

He trained it on The Stallion, only occasionally letting his gaze dart around to try to catch sight of the woman who remained hidden somewhere. The Stallion and Ranger Cooper spoke, back and forth, guns pointed at each other, lawman and madman in the strangest showdown Jaime had ever witnessed.

That gave Jaime the presence of mind to *breathe*. To watch and bide his time. Without knowing where Natalie Torres was, he couldn't act rashly. He—

Something in The Stallion's posture changed and Jaime sighted his gun, ready to shoot, ready to stop The Stallion before anything happened to Ranger Cooper. But before he could line up his shot and pull the trigger without accidentally hitting Cooper, Cooper fired.

The gun flew from The Stallion's hand and he howled with rage. Why the hell hadn't Cooper shot the bastard in the heart? Jaime was about to do just that, but the woman appeared from a crevice in one of the rocks, holding her own weapon up and trained on The Stallion.

She reminded him so much of Gabby it physically hurt. There wasn't an identical resemblance, but it was that determined glint in Natalie's dark eyes that had him thinking about Gabby. If she was safe. If any of them would make it through this in one piece.

He shook that thought away. They would. They all damn well would.

And then Natalie pulled the trigger. She missed, but before Jaime could step out from the outcropping, she'd fired again. Even from Jaime's distance he could see the red bloom on The Stallion's stomach.

"Rodriguez!" he screamed, followed by The Stallion's sad attempt at Spanish. Jaime sighed. He could only hope Cooper recognized him, or that they wouldn't shoot on sight. He could stay there, of course, but it would be worse if he waited for Ranger Cooper to find him.

He stepped out from behind the land swell and walked slowly and calmly toward his writhing fake boss.

Ranger Cooper watched him with the dawning realization of recognition, but Natalie clearly didn't have a clue as she kept her gun trained on him.

Jaime thought maybe, maybe, there was a chance he could maintain his identity and get back to Gabby, so he nodded to Cooper. "Tell your woman to put down the gun," he said in Spanish.

Cooper looked over at the woman. "Put it down, Nat," he murmured, an interesting softness in the command. One Jaime thought he recognized.

Wasn't that odd?

"I won't let anyone kill us. Not now. Not when that man has my sister," Natalie said, her hands shaking, her dark eyes shiny with tears. The Torres women were truly a marvel.

The Stallion made a grab for Jaime's leg piece, but Jaime easily kicked him away. No, he wasn't Rodriguez anymore. He had to be the man he'd always been, and he had to do his duty.

He wasn't Rodriguez, a monster with a shady past. He was Jaime Alessandro, FBI agent, and regardless of *who* he was, he'd find a way to get Gabby to safety as soon as he got out of there.

"Ma'am, I need you to put your weapon down," Jaime said, steady and sure, making eye contact with Natalie. "I'm with the FBI. I've been working undercover for Callihan." Jaime ignored The Stallion's outraged cry, because he saw the way the information tumbled together in Natalie's head.

She didn't even have to ask about Gabby for him to know that's what she needed to hear. "I know where your sister is. She's…safe."

Natalie didn't just lower her gun, she dropped it. She sank to the rocky ground and Jaime had to raise an eyebrow at Ranger Cooper sinking with her.

He couldn't hear what they said to each other, but it didn't matter. He turned to The Stallion. Victor Callihan. The man who'd made his life a living hell for two years.

He was still writhing on the ground, bloody and pale, shaking possibly with shock or with the loss of blood. He might make it. He might not. Jaime supposed it would depend on how quickly they worked.

Jaime slid into a crouch. "How does it feel, *senor*," Jaime mused aloud, "to be so completely outwitted by everyone around you?"

"You think this is over?" The Stallion rasped. "It'll never be over. As long as I *breathe,* you're mine, and it will never, *ever*, be over."

Jaime had been through too much for those words to have any impact. The Stallion thought he could intimidate him? Make him fear? Not in this lifetime or the next.

"There's already an FBI raid at all four of your compounds." He was gratified when the man's eyes bulged. "Oh, did you think I didn't put it together? The southern compound? You know who helped me figure out its location? Ah, no, I don't want to ruin the surprise. I'll let you worry about that. You'll have plenty of time to ruminate in a cell."

The Stallion lunged, but he was weakened and all Jaime had to do was rock back on his heels to avoid the man's grasp.

"Everyone should be out by the time I get back, and you know what my first order of business will be? Burning every last doll in that place," he whispered in the man's ear, before standing.

Jaime turned to Cooper who'd gotten Natalie to her feet. He ignored The Stallion's sputtering and nodded in the direction of the Jeep. "I have rope in my vehicle. We'll tie him up and take him to the closest ranger station."

And then he'd find a way to get to Gabby.

Chapter Fifteen

Gabby stood at the door to her room, Jasmine slightly in front of her. Alyssa and Tabitha had already gone back into the common room, plan in place.

Gabby felt sick, but she pushed it away. The girls were counting on her and so was… Well, she herself. She was the architect of this plan, the leader, and if she wanted them all to survive, she had to be calm and strong.

Jaime was out protecting her sister, and no matter how mad he might be at her for not leaving, she knew he'd do everything to keep Natalie safe.

And she hadn't even told him…

She forced it all away as Alyssa's cue blasted through the house. Gabby exchanged a look with Jasmine. Alyssa was supposed to yell at Tabitha, not scream obscenities at her.

As Gabby and Jasmine slid into the room, Alyssa attacked, stabbing one of her butter knives into Wallace's leg with a brutal force Gabby had to look away from.

Jasmine threw the cords they'd gathered at Tabitha. Wallace screamed in a kind of agony that made Gabby's blood run cold, but she couldn't think about that now. Layne was her target.

His eyes gleamed with an unholy bloodlust and his gun was in his grasp far too fast. But somehow everything seemed to move in slow motion. Before Gabby could even flinch, Jasmine was throwing her body at Layne's legs.

The impact surprised Layne enough that he fell forward, on top of Jasmine, who cried out, mixing with Wallace's screams.

Gabby scrambled forward, pushing Layne off Jasmine so he hit the hard floor on his injured shoulder. He howled in pain, but he didn't let go of the gun as Gabby grabbed it.

She jerked and pulled, but Layne didn't let go. He screamed, but she couldn't wrestle the weapon from his grasp.

Until Jasmine got to her feet and started stomping on his bad shoulder, a wholly different girl than the woman who'd, pale-faced and wide-eyed, told Gabby she wasn't strong enough. Gabby finally wrested the gun free of his hand, trying to think past the high-pitched keening from both men.

"Rope," she gasped then yelled louder.

She glanced at Alyssa and Tabitha. Wallace thrashed, groaning in pain as he swung his hands out, but Tabitha had tied his legs tightly to the chair and Alyssa had already wrestled the gun out of his hands.

Alyssa kicked one of the cords Gabby's way and Gabby grabbed it as Layne tried to scuttle away from Jasmine, cursing and, Gabby thought, maybe even sobbing.

Jasmine stomped another time on his wound, which had now bled completely through his bandage and shirt. His face went white and his eyes rolled back in his head, and it was only then that Gabby realized Jasmine was crying and that Wallace had gone completely silent.

Feeling a sob rise in her throat, Gabby knelt next to Layne and jerked his arms behind his back, doing her best to tie the cord around his thick forearms and wrists. She pulled it as tightly as she possibly could and tied as many knots as the length of cord would allow.

She breathed through her mouth, because something about the smell of Layne—him or his wound—nearly made her woozy.

"I've got his legs," Tabitha said, moving to the end of Layne's lifeless body. Gabby could see the rise and fall of his chest, so he wasn't dead.

She almost wished he was, which was enough to get her to her feet. She glanced back at Alyssa who had ripped off half her shirt and tied it around Wallace's face like a gag. The man still wiggled, but the cords and knots were holding and if he tried to escape too much longer, he'd likely knock the whole chair over.

Alyssa held the gun far too close to Wallace's head.

Gabby crossed to her, holding her hand out for the gun. "Tabitha is going to guard them."

Alyssa didn't spare Gabby a glance. "My suggestion of just killing them stands," she said, her hands tight on the gun, sweat dripping down her temple.

"I need your help to gather evidence."

"They can," Alyssa said, jerking her chin toward Jasmine, who stood with Layne's gun trained on his unmoving form and Tabitha finishing up the knots at his ankles. She never looked at them, just gestured toward them.

"No, I need you," Gabby said firmly.

Alyssa's gaze finally flickered to Gabby. "You need me?"

"Yes. You're the strongest next to me. We'll be able to break down the doors easiest and carry the most stuff. I need you."

Gabby didn't really know if Alyssa was stronger, but it was certainly the most plausible. Clearly it also got through to her since she'd looked away from Wallace.

Maybe it would be easier to kill the men, but Gabby… She didn't want to have to relive that for the rest of her life, and she didn't want the other girls to have to, either.

Alyssa waved the gun a bit. "We might need this to bust the lock off."

Gabby remained steadfast in holding her hand out, palm upward. "Give me the gun, Alyssa. We need to do this as a team."

The woman's mouth turned into a sneer and Gabby thought for sure she'd lost the battle. Any second now Alyssa would pull the trigger and—

She slapped the gun into Gabby's palm. "Let's go get those doors open," she muttered.

Gabby nodded, looking at Tabitha and Jasmine. Jasmine had Layne's gun and Tabitha had what looked to be a dagger of some kind that she must have taken off one of the men.

"Scream if you need anything," Gabby said

sternly. "Once we have whatever evidence we can carry, we'll come get you and lock this place back up, and then we'll start out."

Jasmine and Tabitha nodded, and though they'd handled themselves like old pros, everyone seemed a little shaky now. Far too jumpy. She and Alyssa needed to hurry.

They raced down the hall to the door. "Give me one of those knives."

Alyssa pulled one out of her bra and if Gabby had time she might have marveled at it, but instead she used it to start picking the lock. Turned out Ricky and his ne'er-do-well friends *had* taught her something.

She got the locks free and pushed on the door. It creaked open only a fraction. Alyssa inspected the crack. "It's chained on the outside," she said flatly. "Give me the gun."

Gabby hesitated. "What if it ricochets?"

Alyssa raised an eyebrow. "It won't."

What choice did Gabby have? A butter knife wasn't cutting through chain any more than anything else, and Alyssa might be losing it, but she was sure. They had to be a team.

Gabby handed over the gun. Alyssa shoved the muzzle through the crack, barely managing to fit it, and then a loud shot rang out.

The chain clanked and then after another quick and overly loud shot, Alyssa was pushing the door open.

Both women stumbled into the bright light of day. It very nearly burned, the bright sunshine, the intense blue overhead. Gabby tried to step forward, but only tripped and fell to her knees in the grass.

"Oh, God. Oh, God," Alyssa whispered.

Gabby couldn't see her. Her eyes couldn't seem to adjust to the bright light, and her heart just imploded.

She could smell the grass. She could feel it

under her knees and hands. Hot from the mid-day sun. Rocky soil underneath. It was real. Real and true. The actual earth. Fresh air. The sun. God, the sun.

The one time they'd been let out it had been a cloudy day, and The Stallion hadn't allowed for any reaction. Just digging. But today…today the sun beat down on her face as if it hadn't been missing from her life for eight years.

Gabby tried to hold back the sobs, she had a job to do, after all. A mission, and leaving Tabitha and Jasmine alone with dangerous men no matter how injured or tied up wasn't fair. She had to act.

But all she could seem to do was suck in air and cry.

Then Alyssa's arms were pulling her to her feet. "We have to keep moving, Gabby. We've got time to cry later. Now, we have to move."

Gabby finally managed to blink her eyes

open. Alyssa's jaw was set determinedly and she pointed to a fancy shed in the corner of the yard.

Gabby took a deep breath of air—fresh and sun-laden—and looked down at her hands. She'd grasped some grass and pulled it out, and now it fluttered to the patchy ground below.

The Stallion had kept her from this, *all of this*, for eight long years. It was time to make sure it was his turn to not see daylight for a hell of a lot longer.

JAIME DROVE THE Jeep toward where Cooper's map said there'd be a ranger station. Once they had access to a phone—The Stallion's laptop had been too encrypted to be of use—Jaime would call his superiors and Ranger Cooper's.

Things would be real soon enough, and he still wasn't back to Gabby.

Still, he answered Cooper's questions and

only occasionally glanced at the woman sandwiched between him and the Texas Ranger.

She was slighter than Gabby, certainly softer, and yet she'd been the one to shoot The Stallion as though it had been nothing at all.

Jaime glanced at Cooper's crudely bandaged arm wound. It was bleeding through, though he'd looked over it himself and knew, at most, Cooper would need stitches.

There was an awkward silence between every one of Ranger Cooper's curt questions and every one of Jaime's succinct answers. Tension and stress seemed to stretch between all of them, no matter that The Stallion was apprehended in the back and would likely survive his injuries.

Unless Jaime slowed down. But it wasn't an option, not without news on Gabby and the raid. Too many unknowns, too many possibilities.

He finally found a road after driving through mountains and desert, and soon enough a ranger station came into view. Jaime brought the Jeep to a stop, trying to remember himself and his duty.

He pushed the Jeep into Park and looked at Cooper. "If you stay put, I'll have them call for an ambulance, as well as call your precinct. We'll see if there's any word on the raid to Callihan's house, where your sister was."

Ranger Cooper nodded stoically, putting his hand on his weapon, his glance falling to the back of the Jeep where Victor Callihan, The Stallion, Jaime's tormenter, lay still and tied up.

Bleeding.

Hopefully miserable.

Jaime glanced at Gabby's sister, but she only stared at him. She'd asked no questions about her sister. She'd said almost nothing at all. Jaime figured she was in shock.

"I don't know what to ask," she said, her voice weak and thready.

Jaime gave a sharp nod. "Let me see if I can go find out some basics." He left the Jeep and strode into the station.

A woman behind the counter squeaked, but Jaime held up his hands.

"I'm with the FBI and I need to use your phone." He realized he didn't have his badge, and he still had far too many weapons strapped to his body.

He needed to get his crap together and fast. He kept his hands raised and recited his FBI information. The woman shoved a phone at him, but she backed into a corner of her office and Jaime had no doubt she was radioing for help.

It didn't matter. He called through to his superior, trying to rein in his impatience.

"I'm in a ranger station in the Guadalupe Mountains National Park. I have Texas Ranger Vaughn Cooper and civilian Natalie Torres with me. The Stallion is hurt and disarmed. We need an ambulance for Callihan and Cooper, and I need an immediate debriefing on what's happening at The Stallion's compound in the west."

"Immediate," Agent Lucroy repeated, and though it had been years since Jaime had seen the man in charge of his undercover investigation, he could imagine clearly the man's raised eyebrow. "That's quite the demand."

"Sir," Jaime said, biting back a million things he wanted to yell. "There are four women in that compound, whom I left with armed and dangerous men. It is my duty and my utmost concern that they are safe."

There was a long silence on the line.

"Sir?" Jaime repeated, fearing the worst.

"The raid has been initiated per your message. Our agents are on the ground at the compound..."

"And Ga—the women?"

"Well... Let me get off the phone and contact the necessary authorities to get you out of there. We'll do a proper debriefing when you're back in San Antonio."

Jaime nearly doubled over, fear turning into a nauseating sickness in his gut. Oh, God, he hadn't saved her. She wasn't safe at all.

"What happened to the women?" he demanded. "One of the captives...Natalie Torres, the woman Ranger Cooper has been protecting, she's the sister of one of the captives. She deserves to know..." She deserved to know how horribly he'd failed.

Agent Lucroy sighed. "Let's just say there's a slight...situation at the El Paso compound."

Chapter Sixteen

"Do you think we can carry a computer as far as we need to walk?" Gabby asked, looking dubiously down at the hard drive Alyssa was unhooking from a million monitors.

Alyssa shrugged. "We can get it as far as we need to. Then it's got just as much a chance of being found by whatever cops we can find as any Stallion idiots."

It was a good point. In fact, Alyssa had made quite a few. Though Gabby still didn't trust Alyssa not to go off and do something drastic or dangerous, the woman was very effective under pressure.

They hadn't found any bags or things they could haul evidence in, so they'd shoved any important-looking papers into their pockets. Gabby had come across a map with markings on it, and she thought with enough time she'd be able to figure it out. She'd taken a page out of Alyssa's book and shoved it into her bra.

Gabby went through a shelf of tech gadgets and picked up anything she thought might have memory on it. Anything that could make sure this was over for good.

It's not over until you're out of here.

She tried to ignore the panic beating in her chest and *focus*. "That should be good, don't you think?" When she turned to face Alyssa, the woman was staring at a shelf of dolls. They all looked like variations of the same. Dark hair, unseeing eyes, frilly dresses.

A heavy sense of unease settled over the adrenaline coursing through Gabby. She understood now, completely, why the dolls had weighed so heavily on Jaime. She tried to look away, but it felt as if the dolls were just…staring at—

The shot that rang out made Gabby scream, the doll's head exploding made her wince, but when she wildly looked over at Alyssa, the woman was simply holding the gun up, vaguely smiling.

"Think I have enough bullets to shoot all of them?" she asked conversationally.

"No," Gabby said emphatically. "Let's go. Let's get the hell out of here."

Alyssa nodded, grabbing the computer hard drive and hefting it underneath her arm. She kept the gun in her other hand, but before either of them could make another move, the door burst open.

Gabby dropped to the ground, trying to hide behind the desk that dominated the shed, but Alyssa only turned, gun aimed at the invasion of men.

Men in *uniform*.

"FBI. Put down your weapons," they yelled in chorus.

Gabby scrambled back to her feet, blinking a few times, just to make sure… But there it was in big bold letters.

FBI.

Oh, *God*. She searched the men's faces, but none of them was Jaime.

"Drop your weapon, ma'am," one of them intoned, his voice flat and commanding.

Alyssa stared at the man and most decidedly did *not* drop her weapon.

"Alyssa," Gabby hissed.

"I'm not going to be a prisoner for another second," Alyssa said, her voice deadly calm.

"It's the *FBI*. Look at his uniform, Alyssa. Do what he *says*." Gabby held up her hands, hoping that with her cooperating the men wouldn't shoot.

But Alyssa didn't move. She eyed the FBI agent, both with their weapons raised at each other.

"Ma'am, if you do not lower the weapon, I will be forced to shoot. You have to the count of three. One, two—"

"Ugh, fine," Alyssa relented, lowering her arm. She didn't drop the weapon and she stared at the men with nothing but a scowl.

"They're here to save us," Gabby said, feeling a bubble of hysteria try to break free. She wanted to cry. She wanted to throw herself at these men's feet. She wanted Jaime and to know for sure…

"It's over, isn't it?" she asked, a tear slipping down her cheek.

"Ma'am, you have to drop your weapon. We cannot escort you out of here until you do," he said to Alyssa, ignoring Gabby completely.

"There are two other women inside the house. Did you—?" Gabby had started to step forward, but one of the men held up his hand and she stopped on a dime.

"We will not be discussing anything until she drops her damn weapon," the man said through gritted teeth.

There were four of them, three with their weapons trained on Alyssa, a fourth one behind the three on a phone, maybe relaying information to someone.

Alyssa had her grip on the gun so tight her knuckles were white and Gabby didn't know how to fix this.

"What are you doing?" Gabby demanded. She wanted to go over and shake Alyssa till some sense got through that hard head of hers, but she was afraid to move. They were finally free and Alyssa was going to get them both killed.

That made her a different kind of angry. "Why are you treating us like the criminals?" she demanded of the four men, soldier-stiff and stoic.

"Why won't you drop your weapon?" the agent retorted.

Gabby didn't know how long they stood there. It seemed like forever. Alyssa neither dropped her weapon, nor did the men lower theirs. Seconds ticked on, dolls watching from above, and all Gabby could do was stand there.

Stand there in limbo between prison and freedom. Stand there with the threat of this woman who'd become an ally and a friend dying when they'd come this far.

"Please, Alyssa. Please," Gabby whispered after she didn't know how long. Gabby had spent eight years trying to be strong. Beating any emotion out of herself, but all strength did in this moment was make this standoff continue.

She looked at Alyssa, letting the tears fall from her eyes, letting the emotion shake her voice. "Please, put down the gun," she whispered. "I want you safe when we get out of here. I don't want to have to watch you get hurt. Please, Alyssa, put down the gun."

Alyssa swallowed. She didn't drop the gun, though her grip loosened incrementally.

"We all want this to be over," Gabby said, pushing her advantage as hard as she could. "We all want to go home."

"I don't," Alyssa muttered, but she dropped the gun all the same.

JAIME SUPPOSED THAT someday in the future it would be a point of pride that he'd yelled at his superior over the phone and had to be restrained by three fellow agents, and still retained his job.

But when Agent Lucroy had explained there'd been a standoff—a *standoff*—with two women who had been *captives*, no matter how dangerous he'd felt Alyssa could be, Jaime had lost it.

He'd sworn at his boss. He'd thrown the phone across the ranger station. The only thing that had kept his temper on a leash as they'd waited for the ambulance was the fact that Natalie was Gabby's sister.

She didn't need to be as sick with fear and as stuck as he was.

The being restrained by three fellow agents had come later. When they'd had to forcibly put him on a flight to the field office in San Antonio instead of to Austin with Ranger Cooper and Natalie.

There had been a *slight* altercation once getting off the plane when he'd demanded his car and been refused. In the end, a guy he'd once counted as a friend had had to pull a gun on him.

He'd gotten himself together after that. Mostly. He'd met with his boss and had agreed to go through the mandatory debriefing, psych eval and the like. Sure, maybe only after Agent Lucroy had threatened to have him admitted to a psych ward if he didn't comply.

Semantics.

He was held overnight in the hospital, being poked and prodded and mentally evaluated. When he'd been released, he was supposed to go home. He was supposed to meet his superiors at noon and inform them of everything.

Instead he'd gotten in his car and driven in the opposite direction. He very possibly was risking his job and he didn't give a damn. He should go see his parents, his sister. They were in California, but if he was really going to take a break with reality, shouldn't it be to have them in his sight?

When he'd spoken to Mom on the phone, she'd begged him to come home, and when he'd said he couldn't, she'd said she'd be heading to San Antonio as soon as she could. He'd begged her off. Work. Debriefing.

The truth was… He wasn't ready to be Jaime Alessandro quite yet. He'd neither cut his hair nor shaved his beard. He was neither FBI agent nor Stallion lackey, he was something in between, and no amount of FBI shrinks poking at him would give him the key to step back into his old life.

Not until he saw Gabby. So he drove to Austin. Thanks to Ranger Cooper apparently being unaware that he wasn't supposed to know, Jaime had the information that Gabby was still in the hospital and had yet to be reunited with her family.

When Ranger Cooper had relayed that information, Jaime may have broken a few traffic laws to get to the hospital.

All he needed was to see her, to maybe touch her. Then he could breathe again. Maybe then he could find himself again.

Maybe then he'd forgive her for not getting out when he'd wanted her to.

He did some fast talking, but either the hospital staff was exceptionally good or they'd been forewarned. No amount of flashing his badge or trying to sneak around corners worked.

Eventually security had been called. When one security guard appeared, Jaime laughed. Then another had appeared behind him and he figured they were probably serious.

He wasn't armed, but there were ways he could easily incapacitate these men. He could imagine breaking the one in front's nose, the one in back's arm. This middle-aged, not-in-the-best-of-shape security guard *and* his burly partner. Bam, bam, quick and easy.

It was that uncomfortable realization—that he was pushing too hard, pressing against people who didn't deserve it—that had him softening.

So, when the guards grabbed him by the arms, he let them. He let them push him out the doors and into the waiting room.

"What the hell is your problem, man?" the one guy asked, clearly questioning the truth of his FBI claims.

That was a good enough question. He was acting like a lunatic. Not at all like the FBI agent who had been assigned and willfully taken on the deep undercover operation that had just aided in busting a crime organization that had been hurting the people of this state—and others—for over a decade.

"You come through these doors again, the police will be taking your ass to jail. FBI agent or not."

Jaime inclined his head, straightening his shoulders and then his shirt. "I apologize," he managed to rasp, turning away from the guards only to come face-to-face with two women frowning at him.

"Why are you trying to see my daughter?" the middle-aged woman demanded, her hands shaking, her eyes red as though she'd done nothing but cry for days.

If she was Gabby's mother, perhaps she had.

It was the thing that finally woke him up. Really and fully. Gabby's mother, and a woman who looked to be Gabby's grandmother. He'd assumed Natalie wasn't there, but then she walked in from the hallway carrying two paper cups of coffee.

"Agent Alessandro," she said, stopping short. "Did something hap—?"

"No, Ms. Torres. I merely came by to check on your sister, and I was informed, uh…" He glanced at the women who'd likely seen him get tossed out on his ass. "She wasn't seeing visitors."

Natalie handed off the drinks to the other two women, offering a small and weak smile. "She's asked not to see anyone for a bit longer yet, from what the doctor told me."

"And her, uh, health? It's…"

"As good as can be expected. Maybe better. They've had a psychiatrist talking to her a bit. Are you here to question her? I'm not sure—"

"The case we're building against The Stallion will take time, but your sister's contributions… Well, we'll certainly work with her comfort as much as we can."

He looked at the three women who'd been through their own kind of hell. He didn't know them. Maybe they'd spent eight years certain Gabby was dead. Maybe they'd hoped for her return every night for however many nights she'd been gone.

Gabby would know. She'd be able to figure out the math in a heartbeat, or maybe it was her heartbeat, every second away from her family.

A family who had loved her and taken care of her for twenty years. A family who had far more claim to her than the man who'd spent a week with her and left her behind.

He straightened his shirt again, clearing his throat. He pulled out his wallet, a strange sight. It held his ID with his real name. His badge. Things that belonged to Jaime Alessandro, not Rodriguez.

He blinked for a few seconds, forgetting what he was doing.

"Do you want me to call some—?"

He thrust his business card at Natalie, effectively cutting off her too kind offer. "If you need anything, anything at all, any of you, please don't hesitate to contact me. I'll be back in San Antonio for at least another day or two, but it's an easy enough drive."

Natalie looked at him with big brown eyes that looked too much like Gabby's for his shaky control.

"I want all three of you to know how strong Gab—Gabriella was during this whole ordeal," he forced himself to say, feeling stronger and more sure with every word. FBI agent to the last. "She saved herself, and those women, and did an amazing amount of work in allowing us to confidently press charges against a very dangerous man."

She'd been a warrior, a goddess, an immeasurable asset and ally. She was a *survivor* in every iteration of the word, and he wasn't worthy of her. Not like this.

That meant he had to face his responsibilities and figure out how to come back as just that.

Worthy of Gabby.

Chapter Seventeen

Gabby sat in a sterile hospital room dreading the seconds that ticked by. Every second brought her closer to something she didn't know how to face.

Life.

Her family was in the waiting room. She'd been cleared by both the doctor and the psychiatrist to see them. To be released from the hospital. There'd be plenty of therapy and police interviews in the future, but for the most part she could go home.

What did that even mean? Eight years she'd

been missing. Eight years for her family to change. Daddy was gone. Who knew where Mom and Grandma lived. Surely, Natalie had her own life.

Gabby sat on the hospital bed and tried not to hold on to it for dear life when the nurse arrived. Gabby didn't want to leave this room. She didn't want to face whatever waited for her out there.

She'd rather go back to the compound.

It was that thought, and the shuddering denial that went through her, that reminded her… Well, this would be hard, of course it would be. It would be painful, and a struggle, but it was better. So much better than being a prisoner.

"Your family is waiting," the nurse said kindly. "I've got your copy of the discharge papers and the referrals from the psychiatrist. Is there anything you'd like me to relay to your family for you?"

Gabby shook her head, forcing herself to climb off the bed and onto her own two feet. Her own two feet, which had gotten her this far.

She took a shaky breath and followed the nurse out of the safety of her hospital room. The corridor was quiet save for machine beeps and squeaky shoes on linoleum floors. Gabby thought she might throw up, and then they'd probably take her back to a room and she could…

But they reached the doors and the nurse paused, offering a comforting smile. "Whenever you're ready, sweetheart."

Gabby straightened. She'd never be ready, so taking a second was only delaying the inevitable. "Let's go."

The nurse opened the doors and stepped out, Gabby following by some sheer force of will that had gotten her through eight years of hell.

The nurse walked toward three women sitting huddled together. None of them looked *familiar* and yet Gabby knew exactly who they were. Grandma, Mom, Natalie. Older and different and yet *them.*

Natalie got to her feet, her face white and her eyes wide as though she were looking at a ghost.

Gabby felt like one. Natalie reached out, but it was almost blindly, as if she didn't know what she was reaching for. As if Gabby were really a vision Natalie's hand would simply move through.

Her little sister. A woman in her own right. Eight years lost between them, and she was reaching out for a ghost. But Gabby was no ghost.

"Nattie." It was out of her mouth before Gabby'd even thought it. She grabbed Natalie's hand and squeezed it. Real. Alive. Her sister. Flesh and bone and *soul*. They weren't the same women anymore, but they were still sisters. No matter what separated them.

Natalie didn't say anything, just gaped at her. Mom and Grandma were still sitting, sobbing openly and loudly. Two women she'd barely ever seen cry. The Torres family kept their *sadness* on the down low or hidden in anger, but never…

Never this.

"Say something," Gabby whispered to Natalie, desperate for something to break this tight bubble of pain inside her.

"I don't know…" Natalie sucked in a deep breath, looking up at Gabby who remained an inch or two taller. "I'm so sorr—"

Gabby shook her head and cupped Natalie's face with her hands. She would fall apart with apologies from innocent bystanders. "No, none of that."

Natalie let out a sob and her entire body leaned into Gabby. A hug. Tears over her. Gabby didn't sob, but her own tears slid down her cheeks as she held her sister back.

Real. Not a dream. Nothing but *real*. She glanced over Natalie's head at her mother and grandmother. She held an arm out to them. "Mama, Grandma." Her voice was little more than a rasp, but she used as commanding a tone as she could muster. "Come here."

It only took a second before they were on their feet, wrapping their arms around her, holding on too tightly, struggling to breathe through tears and hugs.

Gabby shook, something echoing all the way through her body so violently she couldn't fight it off. It was relief. It was fear. It was her mother's arms wrapped tight around her.

"Are you all right?" Natalie asked, clearly

concerned over Gabby's shaking. "Do you need a doctor? I'll go get the nu—"

But Gabby held her close. "I'm all right, baby sister. I just can't believe it's real. You're all here."

"They...told you about...Daddy?"

Gabby swallowed, her chin coming up, and she did her best to harden her heart. She'd deal with the softer side of that grief some other time. "The Stallion made sure I knew."

"But..."

Gabby shook her head. She shouldn't have mentioned that man, that evil. She was free, and she wasn't going back to that place. "No. Not today. Maybe not ever."

"One of us needs to get it together so we can drive home," Mama said, her hand shaking as she mopped up tears. Her other hand was a death grip around Gabby's elbow. Gabby didn't even try to escape it. It was like an anchor. A truth.

"I'm all right," Natalie assured them. "I'll drive. Right now. We're free to go. We're… Let's get out of here. And go home."

"Home," Gabby echoed. What was home? She supposed she'd find out soon enough. But as they turned to leave the waiting room, someone entered, blocking the way.

Gabby's heart felt as though it stopped beating for a good moment. She barely recognized him. He'd had a haircut and a shave and today looked every inch the FBI agent in his suit and sunglasses.

She stiffened, because she wasn't ready for this, because her first instinct was to throw herself at him.

Because an angry slash of hurt wound through her. He hadn't come to check on her, and no one had told her what had happened to him.

She'd been afraid to ask. Afraid he'd be dead. Afraid he'd been a figment of her imagination. So afraid of everything outside these walls.

Now he was just *here*, looking polished and perfect. Not Jaime, but the man he'd been before the compound. A man she didn't know and…

She didn't know how to do *all* of this today, so she threw her shoulders back and greeted him coolly, no matter how big a mess she must look from all the crying.

"Ms. Torres."

Even his voice was different, as though the man she'd known in the compound simply hadn't existed. That had been a beating fear inside her for days and now it was a reality.

She could only fight it with a strength she was faking.

His gaze took her in quickly then moved to her sister. "Ms.….well, Natalie, I've got a message for you."

Gabby's grip tightened on Natalie's arm, though she didn't dare show a hint of the fear beating against her chest.

"It's from the Texas Rangers' office."

It was Natalie's turn to grip, to stiffen. Jaime held out a piece of paper and Natalie frowned at it. "They couldn't have called me? Sent an email?" she muttered.

Jaime's gaze was on Gabby and she just… had to look away.

"Agent Alessandro, would you be able to escort Gabby and my family home while I see to this?"

Gabby whipped her head to her sister, whose expression was…angry, Gabby thought. She thought she recognized that stubborn anger on her sister's face.

"I'd love to be of service," Jaime said. "But I doubt your sister…"

He was trying to beg off because of *her*? Oh, no. Hell, no. "Oh, no, please escort us, Mr. *Alessandro*. *I* don't have a problem with it in the least," Gabby replied, linking arms with Mama and Grandma.

He didn't get to run away anymore.

Gabby saw the uncertainty on Natalie's face, but Gabby wanted to be done. Done with law enforcement and the past eight years. "Tie up loose ends, sissy. I want this over, once and for all," she said, not bothering to even look at Jaime.

"It will be," Natalie promised before she stalked past Jaime.

When Gabby finally looked at Jaime, his eyebrows were drawn together, some emotion shuttered in his expression. She couldn't read it. She didn't want to.

He didn't want anything to do with her now. Couldn't even stand to be in her presence? Well, she'd prove that she didn't care about him at all, no matter that it was a lie.

DRIVING GABBY AND her mother and grandmother home was very much not on Jaime's list of things to do today. It, in fact, went against everything he was *trying* to do.

The FBI psychiatrist he'd been forced to talk to had insisted that any relationship with Gabby had been born of the situation and not actual feeling.

Jaime didn't buy it. He was too seasoned an officer, had been in too many horrible situations. He knew for a fact Gabby was just *different*.

But the problem was that Gabby wasn't a seasoned officer. She was a woman who'd been a kidnapping victim for eight years, and no matter what he felt or what he was sure of, she had a whole slew of things to work through that had nothing to do with him.

He'd only meant to relay the message from Ranger Cooper to Natalie. Not…see Gabby. With her family. The same woman he'd shared a bed with only a few days ago, before the strange world they'd been living in imploded.

She'd been crying, it was clear. He'd had to stand there, forcing himself not to take another step, for fear he would grab her away from all of them.

He glanced over at her sitting in his passenger seat. She was in his car. *His* car. In the daylight. Real and breathing next to him.

Her eyes were on the road, her profile to him, chin raised as though the road before them was a sea of admirers she was deigning to acknowledge.

He wanted to stop the car and demand she

tell him everything, forget the fact her mother and grandmother were in the back.

But those women remained a good reminder of what had knocked him out of the raging idiot who'd nearly gotten himself fired and ruined the rest of his life. Women who'd truly suffered, nearly as much as Gabby, in the loss of her.

She deserved the time and space to rebuild with her family first. He didn't have any place in that. He would drive her home and…

He had to grip the wheel tighter because if he thought about leaving her at her house and just driving away…

But he'd made his decision. He'd made the *right* choice. He would keep his distance. He would give her time to heal. If she… Well, if she eventually came to him… He had to give her the space to make the first move.

You know that's stupid.

He ground his teeth together. No matter how stupid he *thought* it was, he was trying to do the right thing for Gabby. That's what was important.

"Natalie tells us you were undercover with the evil man?" Gabby's grandmother asked from the back seat.

"Yes." He turned onto the street Gabby's mother had named when they'd started. He didn't realize he'd slowed down to almost a crawl until someone honked from behind.

"It's the blue one on the corner," the grandmother supplied.

Jaime nodded and hit the accelerator. No matter that he didn't want to let Gabby out of the car, it was his duty. More, it was what she needed. Her family. Her life.

It would be a difficult transition for her, and he didn't need to make that any more complicated for her. It was the right thing to do.

No matter how completely wrong it felt.

He pulled his car into the driveway of a small, squat, one-story home. It looked well kept, if a little sagging around the edges.

Gabby blinked at it and it took every last ounce of control he had not to reach over and brush his mouth across the soft curve of her cheek. Not to touch her and comfort her.

She looked young and lost, and he wanted to protect her from all that swamp of emotion she'd be struggling with.

"I got written up," he blurted into the silence of the car.

What the hell are you doing?

He didn't know. He needed to stop.

"You…" Gabby blinked at him, cocking her head.

"I think they gave me a little leeway what with just being out of undercover and all, but they don't take kindly to ignoring orders."

Shut your mouth and let her go, idiot.

"You…ignored orders," she repeated, as though she didn't quite believe it.

"They told me not to come to the hospital. Or try to see you. I may have…" He cleared his throat and turned his attention to the house in front of them. "I may have caused a bit of a scene."

"He got kicked out by security guards that first morning you were in the hospital," Grandma offered from the back. "A little rougher around the edges that day."

Jaime flicked a silencing glance in the rear-view at the grandma. She smiled sweetly. "Natalie said you must have spent some time together when you were both in that place. Did you take care of our Gabriella?"

Gabby stiffened.

"I tried," Jaime said, perhaps a little too much of his still simmering irritation bleeding through. *If* she had come with him, she wouldn't have been in that standoff with Alyssa. They would have had… They could have…

"Mama, Grandma, will you…give me a few minutes alone with Agent Alessandro?" Gabby asked, her voice soft if commanding.

"Gabriella…" Her mother reached over the seat and put a hand to Gabby's shoulder.

"Gabby, please. Only Gabby from now on," Gabby whispered, eyes wide and haunted and not looking back at her mother.

"Come inside, baby. We'll—"

"I just need a few minutes alone. I promise. Only a few." She looked back at her mother and offered a smile.

But he was supposed to be giving her space. Not…alone time. "You should go—"

Gabby sent him a glare that would have

silenced pretty much anyone, Jaime was pretty sure.

"Come now, Rosa," the grandmother said, patting the mother's arm. "Let's let these two talk. We'll go make some tea for our Gabri— Gabby."

Gabby's mother brushed a hand over Gabby's hair, but reluctantly agreed. The two women slid out of the back of his car and walked up to the house with a few nervous glances back.

Gabby's gaze followed them, an unaccountable hurt languishing in her dark brown eyes. He kept his hands on the wheel so he wouldn't be tempted to touch her.

"So…" Jaime said when Gabby just stared at him for long, ticking seconds. "How are you feeling?"

She didn't answer, just kept staring at him with that hauntingly unreadable gaze.

"Well, I, uh, have things to do," he forced

himself to say, wrenching his gaze from searching her face for signs of things that were none of his business.

"Take off your sunglasses," she said in return.

"Gabby—"

She reached over and yanked them off his face with absolutely no finesse. "Hey!"

"You look different," she stated matter-of-factly.

"A haircut and a shave will do that to a man," he returned, still not meeting her shrewd gaze. He had a mission. A job. A duty. Not for him, but for her. For *her*.

"You look *scared*."

"Scared?" he scoffed, despite the overhard beating of his heart. "I hardly think—"

"Then look at me."

Scared? No. He wasn't scared. He was strong and capable of doing his duty. He was a reliable and excellent FBI agent. He could face down a man with guns and evil, he could certainly face a woman—

Aw, hell, the second he looked at her he had to touch. He had to pull her into his arms despite the console between them. He had to fit his mouth to hers and *feel* as much as know she was there, she was alive, she was safe.

He brushed his hands over her hair, her cheeks, her arms, assuring himself she was real. Her fingers traced his clean-shaved jaw, over the bristled ends of his hair, as she kissed him back with a sweetness and fervency he wasn't supposed to allow.

"I'm not supposed to be doing this," he murmured against her lips, managing to take his mouth from hers only to find his lips trailing down her neck.

"Why not?" she asked breathlessly, her hands smoothing across his back.

"Space and…healing stuff."

"I don't want space. And if I'm going to go through all the shit of healing, I at least want you."

He focused on the edge of the console currently digging into his thigh, because if he focused on that instead of kissing her in daylight, real and free, he might survive.

He managed to find her shoulders, pull her back enough that her hands rested on his forearms.

Flushed and tumbled. From him.

"I'm supposed to give you space," he said firmly, a reminder to himself far more than a response to her.

"I don't want it," she said, her fingers curling around his arms. "And I think I deserve what I want for a bit."

She deserved *everything*. But he wanted to make sure giving it to her was…right. Safe.

"I've had to see a psychiatrist, and there's some…mandatory psychological things I'll have to do before I'm reinstated to active duty. I'm sure the doctor suggested the same thing to you."

"Therapy, yes."

"There's a chance…" He cleared his throat and smoothed his hands down her arms, eventually taking her hands in his.

That wasn't fair because how did he say anything he needed to when he was touching her? "You shouldn't feel *obligated* to continue what happened in there. You should have the space to find out if it's what you really want."

She cocked her head, some mix of irritation and uncertainty in the move. "Do *you* feel obligated by what happened?" she asked.

"No, but—"

"Then shut up." Then her mouth was on his

again, hot and maybe a little wild. But it didn't matter, did it?

He didn't want it to matter. He wanted her. This strong, resilient woman.

She pulled back a little, always his warrior, facing whatever hard things were in her way. "I want you. The Jaime I met in there. And I want to get to know this you," she said, running her finger down the lapel of his suit. "The thing is, awful things happened in there, but it was eight years of my life. I can't…erase it. It's there. Forever. An indelible part of me. I don't need to pretend it never existed to heal. I don't think that's *how* you heal."

"But I have this whole life to go back to, Gabby. I know you aren't starting over, but people knew I was coming back. I'm coming back to a job. It isn't the same space we're in. I don't want you to feel as though you need to make space for me. That…you need to love me or any of it."

She studied him for the longest time, and the marvelous thing about Gabby was that she thought about things. Thought them through, and gave everything the kind of weight it deserved.

Who was he to tell her she needed space? Who was he to tell her much of anything?

"I will tell you when I need space. You'll tell me when you need some. It's not complicated." She traced a fingertip along his hairline, as though studying this new facet to him. Eventually her eyes met his.

"And I do love you," she said quietly, weighted. "If that changes, I'd hardly feel obligated to keep giving you something I didn't have."

"Such a pragmatist," he managed to say, his

voice rusty in the face of her confession. "I was trying to be very noble, you know."

Her mouth curved and he wondered how many things he would file away in his memories as *first in daylight*. The first time he'd kissed her with the sun shining into the car. The first smile under a blue sky.

He wanted them to outnumber his memories of a cramped room more than he wanted his next breath.

"I don't want noble. I want Jaime." She swallowed. "That is, as long as you want me."

"I practically lost my life's work for wanting you, and I'd do it a million times over, if that's what you wanted. I'd give up anything. I'd fight anything. I hope you know, I'd do *anything.*"

She rubbed her hands up and down his cheeks as if to make sure he was real, and hers, though he undoubtedly was. Always.

"Come inside. I want to tell my mother and grandmother about the man who saved me."

"I didn't—"

"You did. I'd stopped counting the days. I'd stopped hoping. You came in and gave me both."

His chest ached, a warm bloom of emotion. Touched that anything he'd done had mattered. Moved beyond measure. "We saved each other." Because he'd been falling, losing all those pieces of himself, and she'd brought it all back.

"A mutual saving. I like that." She smiled that beautiful sun-drenched smile and then she got out of his car, and so did he. They walked up the path to her home with a bright blue sky above them, free and ready for a future.

Together.

* * * * *

MILLS & BOON®
Large Print – September 2017

ROMANCE

The Sheikh's Bought Wife	Sharon Kendrick
The Innocent's Shameful Secret	Sara Craven
The Magnate's Tempestuous Marriage	Miranda Lee
The Forced Bride of Alazar	Kate Hewitt
Bound by the Sultan's Baby	Carol Marinelli
Blackmailed Down the Aisle	Louise Fuller
Di Marcello's Secret Son	Rachael Thomas
Conveniently Wed to the Greek	Kandy Shepherd
His Shy Cinderella	Kate Hardy
Falling for the Rebel Princess	Ellie Darkins
Claimed by the Wealthy Magnate	Nina Milne

HISTORICAL

The Secret Marriage Pact	Georgie Lee
A Warriner to Protect Her	Virginia Heath
Claiming His Defiant Miss	Bronwyn Scott
Rumours at Court (Rumors at Court)	Blythe Gifford
The Duke's Unexpected Bride	Lara Temple

MEDICAL

Their Secret Royal Baby	Carol Marinelli
Her Hot Highland Doc	Annie O'Neil
His Pregnant Royal Bride	Amy Ruttan
Baby Surprise for the Doctor Prince	Robin Gianna
Resisting Her Army Doc Rival	Sue MacKay
A Month to Marry the Midwife	Fiona McArthur

MILLS & BOON®
Hardback – October 2017

ROMANCE

Claimed for the Leonelli Legacy	Lynne Graham
The Italian's Pregnant Prisoner	Maisey Yates
Buying His Bride of Convenience	Michelle Smart
The Tycoon's Marriage Deal	Melanie Milburne
Undone by the Billionaire Duke	Caitlin Crews
His Majesty's Temporary Bride	Annie West
Bound by the Millionaire's Ring	Dani Collins
The Virgin's Shock Baby	Heidi Rice
Whisked Away by Her Sicilian Boss	Rebecca Winters
The Sheikh's Pregnant Bride	Jessica Gilmore
A Proposal from the Italian Count	Lucy Gordon
Claiming His Secret Royal Heir	Nina Milne
Sleigh Ride with the Single Dad	Alison Roberts
A Firefighter in Her Stocking	Janice Lynn
A Christmas Miracle	Amy Andrews
Reunited with Her Surgeon Prince	Marion Lennox
Falling for Her Fake Fiancé	Sue MacKay
The Family She's Longed For	Lucy Clark
Billionaire Boss, Holiday Baby	Janice Maynard
Billionaire's Baby Bind	Katherine Garbera

0917 GEN STD HB

MILLS & BOON®
Large Print – October 2017

ROMANCE

Sold for the Greek's Heir	Lynne Graham
The Prince's Captive Virgin	Maisey Yates
The Secret Sanchez Heir	Cathy Williams
The Prince's Nine-Month Scandal	Caitlin Crews
Her Sinful Secret	Jane Porter
The Drakon Baby Bargain	Tara Pammi
Xenakis's Convenient Bride	Dani Collins
Her Pregnancy Bombshell	Liz Fielding
Married for His Secret Heir	Jennifer Faye
Behind the Billionaire's Guarded Heart	Leah Ashton
A Marriage Worth Saving	Therese Beharrie

HISTORICAL

The Debutante's Daring Proposal	Annie Burrows
The Convenient Felstone Marriage	Jenni Fletcher
An Unexpected Countess	Laurie Benson
Claiming His Highland Bride	Terri Brisbin
Marrying the Rebellious Miss	Bronwyn Scott

MEDICAL

Their One Night Baby	Carol Marinelli
Forbidden to the Playboy Surgeon	Fiona Lowe
A Mother to Make a Family	Emily Forbes
The Nurse's Baby Secret	Janice Lynn
The Boss Who Stole Her Heart	Jennifer Taylor
Reunited by Their Pregnancy Surprise	Louisa Heaton

MILLS & BOON®

Why shop at millsandboon.co.uk?

Each year, thousands of romance readers find their perfect read at millsandboon.co.uk. That's because we're passionate about bringing you the very best romantic fiction. Here are some of the advantages of shopping at www.millsandboon.co.uk:

* **Get new books first**—you'll be able to buy your favourite books one month before they hit the shops

* **Get exclusive discounts**—you'll also be able to buy our specially created monthly collections, with up to 50% off the RRP

* **Find your favourite authors**—latest news, interviews and new releases for all your favourite authors and series on our website, plus ideas for what to try next

* **Join in**—once you've bought your favourite books, don't forget to register with us to rate, review and join in the discussions

Visit **www.millsandboon.co.uk**
for all this and more today!